Nicole Stone lives in the beautiful Finger Lakes region of Upstate NY with her two kids, husband, dog, and cat. While she isn't writing she is reading a good book, hiking the many beautiful waterfalls, or painting with her daughter. She spends her time discussing her son's latest favorite book with him and going to NFL games with her husband.

Nicole Stone

SOULS TOGETHER

Thanks for the Support

AUSTIN MACAULEY PUBLISHERS™

LONDON • CAMBRIDGE • NEW YORK • SHARJAH

Ordering Information
Quantity sales: Special discounts are available on quantity purchases by corporations, associations, and others. For details, contact the publisher at the address below.

Publisher's Cataloging-in-Publication data
Stone, Nicole
Souls Together

ISBN 9781641823616 (Paperback)
ISBN 9781641829342 (Hardback)
ISBN 9781643785585 (ePub e-book)

Library of Congress Control Number: 2021906324

www.austinmacauley.com/us

First Published (2021)
Austin Macauley Publishers LLC
40 Wall Street, 33rd Floor, Suite 3302
New York, NY 10005
USA

mail-usa@austinmacauley.com
+1 (646) 5125767

Prologue

"You're a witch, Serena."

"What?!" I say to my mother...waiting for the punch line. This has to be a joke, right? That was not what I was expecting to hear on the morning of my 18th birthday.

Sure we live in a small town with more cows than people, and yes, we don't have a lot of money. But really a car would have been nice, and not a joke.

"We aren't joking, honey," my mom, Diana, says with an apologetic look on her beautiful face.

My parents don't look crazy. Does crazy show? Is it like hives? Maybe a twitching eye? I look over to them, looking them up and down. They look as they always do. My mom looks like me; well, maybe I look like her. Our brown hair that never looks brown. With streaks of red, blonde, and even some black, our hair changes with different light. Our eyes are a bright green that sometimes seem to glow. My friends are always so jealous. We have high cheek bones, a petite nose, and full lips. Yes, I know I'm a genetically lucky bitch; if it makes you feel better, I am really short, like five-nothing short. Okay, so maybe not that bad but still, no modeling career for this girl.

My dad, well, he's the odd ball with blonde hair and blue eyes, and classically strong features. My friends think he is the hottest thing though. *Insert gag here*.

No, they don't look crazy. No dilation of the pupils. No hives. No twitching eyes. They look serious. Which, really, is worse.

I can't do this today. Not only is it my 18th birthday, but it is the first day of senior year. I need to focus or go get a lotto ticket. I haven't decided yet. I have decided that I really do not want to deal with this right now, so I jump up off the couch. "I have to go to school. Can't be late on the first day of my senior year," I say as I start backing out of the living room to the front door.

I grab my bag off the table by the door as I all but run out of the house, ignoring my parents as they yell after me. "Serena, no, you need to listen! We are not joking about this, Serena!" On the porch, I come to an abrupt halt as what my mom said catches up to me. Did she tell me that they weren't joking as if I said they were? Twice she did that. I never said I thought they were out loud, only in my head. Come to think of it…my mom has always had an uncanny way of just knowing things and of just appearing. I swear she is the sneakiest person I have ever known. I give my head a shake, she probably just assumed I thought that. Who wouldn't, right? And why would this one time stand out to me so much? She has always said what I am thinking…

I'm a witch? What…? I shake my head, I can't right now.

Chapter 1

Just then Sam pulls up. This is normal, so apparently, the entire world has not fallen of its rocker. I walk over to the car and smile.

This morning is a little different, the car is stuffed full of balloons. Sam always knows how to make me laugh.

"Hey, Sam!" I giggle as I try to sit in the front seat and not be attacked or choked by balloons.

"HAPPY BIRTHDAY!!!" Sam yells as loud as she possibly can. I can't help but laugh. Sam is the most enthusiastic person I have ever met, and in such a small body. Sam Evans is a gorgeous girl at 5'2" and 105 pounds, with long golden hair and big blue eyes. She is the girl other girls hate because she never gets a ticket. With a bat of her eyes and a sweet smile, Sam can get anything. She is the sweetest and most loving person. Yet she is not someone you want to piss off, trust me. Guys would call her a bomb shell, well, I mean it literally. When Sam gets angry, she is like a bomb going off; luckily it takes a lot to get her that worked up.

"Thanks, Sam! This is so sweet." I say looking at the back seat full of balloons trying to make a break to the front. I laugh again shaking my head as I fight them back.

"No problem, only the best for my bestie! So, what did your parents get you?" Sam asks as she pulls out of the driveway.

"I don't know, I was running late so I didn't really talk to them," I lie; she of course knows that I am lying. I know I am the worst friend in the world, but I am not repeating the talk I had with my parents. I am starting to think they were being serious. Which means I may need to check them into the hospital psych ward for observation. *You're a witch, Serena.* What does that even mean? Witches aren't real. Just like werewolves and vampires and gremlins aren't real.

My parents are pagan. But not once in my life have I heard them call themselves witches.

But why would they even say that if they weren't telling the truth. *You're a witch* is a really bad joke. What would the punch line be? Get on your broomstick because here comes the wort?

I am so deep in thought over this morning that I miss the whole car ride to school. "Sorry, Sam, I didn't hear anything you said."

"I know, I just figured you were day-dreaming about the car your parents got you." Sam laughed.

"They got me a car?" I ask jumping in my seat to look at her as she turns the key.

"I don't know, sorry, I am just hoping. Not that I don't love giving you a ride to school, because I do, but I know you want your own. Who doesn't, right?" Sam says, giving me a hopeful look. Sam has a '03 Ford Focus that belonged to her mom until this past July. Her mom told her that as long as Sam pays the insurance, the car was hers. Lucky.

"I actually like riding in with you. But yes, I would rather drive myself." We walk to the gym entrance and head up the stairs to our lockers. Since we are seniors this year, we get the secluded lockers over the gym lobby. As freshmen, this hallway was like a secret society. With only one class room that is a senior English class, and the halls that run the length of the school ending in this hall, only seniors come down here.

I head to my locker and unpack my bag, soaking in the moment. A senior. This was it and then my life can really begin.

Before I head over to meet Sam at the end of the hall, I check my schedule one last time. Not a very full schedule this year, YAY… sarcasm, my strongest skill that never fades but only grows stronger. At least I have a backup plan, politics, I just need to work on my lying skills.

"I am so happy this is the last time I spend my birthday on the first day of school. At least in college I will have been in school for a month and be settled," I say to Sam as I reach her and we start walking to class.

"Happy birthday!" she says, again. This time in a hopeful, please-smile-and-be-happy voice.

"Yup, already tired of it," I say as I roll my eyes at her.

"Okay, cheer up," Sam says coming to a halt half way down the hall. "You are 18 today! You should be happy! Think of all the things you can do now! You can vote, buy lottery tickets…" she pauses in the middle of another thing I can now do as an 18-year-old. Only there isn't anything else. "Okay, not much more than that, but still amazing!! Tonight, how about we take a drive to Ithaca and catch a movie or something?"

"As awesome as that sounds, I think I should go home. You know, birthday dinner with the parents. Tomorrow though?" I ask giving her a pleading look.

Sam laughs as she says, "Okay, tomorrow, but you owe me since it will no longer be your birthday!"

"Ha-ha, birthday week still counts," I say as she rolls her eyes at me with a smile. The warning bell rings and we head are separate ways.

My first class is accounting; I groan a very painful groan. This means I get the wonderful start of math every day! I hate math, well actually, math hates me. I try, I really do. I study till my brain hurts, I ask questions, I have even been known to stay after school for one-on-one time. I still just cannot grasp any sort of math. I am not sure why I am taking accounting. I finished all my math credits last year. But if I don't take some sort of math, I will forget how to add. Yeah, I am that bad.

Mrs. Cornwell has us all grab a workbook off her desk and check our names off the attendance sheet before we take our seats. Of course, I sit in the back behind Greg Lorscky; being six two, he is the best chance I have at becoming invisible or at the very least, hard to see.

After ten minutes of my first day, I am completely lost. I can tell already, I am going to LOVE this class! *Insert sarcasm here*.

As normal, when talking about math, my mind wanders. Yes, I have given up any hope of being a mathematician or even balancing my check book. I am okay with this.

I have American History, then English, two very easy classes after Accounting. Luckily, I opted not to take an extra science this year but that leaves me with a free period before lunch. Honestly, I am wondering if I made the right choice by not graduating early. I had that option last year. I didn't want to leave my friends, but I have a lot of free time this year because of it. Oh well, I am here now.

I am just feeling this way because it is the first day and I am still freaking out over this morning's events. I just need to get through a few more classes, then I can meet up with Sam and I can be distracted for a little while. And with that mental breakdown of my classes and a short muse of my decision-making skills, I have missed half of class. Awesome.

I meet up with Sam at lunch and she is already freaking out, "Can you believe that we have all this homework already? I mean really, can we at least have a day to get our bearings." Sam is so very dramatic, that comes in handy for the school plays, and she is doing her job of distracting me very well.

"While you freak out over that, I will freak out over the fact that we have four more periods and two of those are study halls for me and I have already had one. Oh, and the two classes I have are Gym and Chorus. So, no homework for me," I add just because I knew I would get Sam to turn to me and give me her *I will kill you* look. Which of course makes me laugh hysterically.

That look scares most people; okay, it makes them cower in fear. Sam may look like a poke would send her flying but her tongue is sharper than any blade. To make it worse, she has this way of looking at a person and just knowing what to say to hurt them the most.

"Aren't you lucky then, you wouldn't be this calm and relaxed about all the homework if you hadn't taken half of this year's classes last year. Wait…what happened to you taking college courses?" Sam asks. I really don't want to talk about it, but Sam won't let it go until I do…

"I tried to save up for the classes because my parents had to use what they had saved to fix the greenhouse but then they said they would go halves on a car for me and that is a little more important right now. Still, I am hoping that they will surprise me with a car so I can use the money for classes." Though I don't see that happening.

We get our food and go sit outside with Jenny, a curly-haired, freckle-faced girl. We have been 'friends' with Jenny for years. I say that, but we really have never hung out with her outside of school. Jenny is shy, that explains that.

Since it is a warm and sunny day, we can sit at the picnic tables outside. Normally we sit next to the windows in the center of the cafeteria. Living in the second most rainy region in the United States can sometimes put a damper on outdoor enjoyment.

Sara and her boyfriend, James, are also already at the table. I was really hoping that relationship had ended over the summer but I see that it didn't; really, I should have already known that. Sara is, or was, mine and Sam's best friend since the 3rd grade, but last year when she started dating James, that changed. James is rich, smart, and cute; the bad of all that is he knows it. He treats Sara like she should owe him for dating her. Enough said.

We sit down and listen to Sara and James's stories of their summer together as if we want to. Sam gives me bored looks all through lunch that I try not to laugh at, and fail.

Of course, I then get daggers thrown at me from James. Which, of course, I can't help but make worse by giving him the 'that is the worst look you have, well you don't scare me look.' Really, the guy is a pig. I'm not sure what she sees in him. Sara could do so much better. I really wish she would dump his butt and not just because he is a jerk. We are young, with our entire lives to settle down, why waste our time now? This is our senior year of high school, we should be spending it together. The three of us, having the time of our lives. Instead, Sam and I are sitting here listening to James the Jerk, wishing we were somewhere else.

I miss Sara. She was always the life of the party. She brought Sam and I out of our shells. It was always just us. Until we met Sara; she dragged us to the other kids at recess and made us play. She always brought us into the light.

Finally, lunch ends and we say goodbye to the lovely couple *Insert sarcasm here*.

I have Chorus after lunch, my favorite class because it is the only class I end up having with Sam. It is as if the teachers know that if Sam and I have a class together, we will be a disruption to all. Where they got that idea from, I have no clue.

We warmed up, then talked about the plans for this year and sang a few old songs. Sam and I spent the class talking. I know, bad Serena. This class may be how they know...

I have two more study halls before my last class of the day, Gym. Crap, I think I forgot gym clothes. On the bright side, we never start out with some sort of sport on the first day. We always discuss what we will be doing all year. Which is always the same thing: square dance, mile run, track, soccer, field hockey, and so on. Luckily, I don't need a change of clothes.

Since I have already done all my homework during my first study hall, I walk over to the library and grab some new books to read. I sit at one of the tables next to the windows overlooking the office. Really, I should go over my Accounting book and try to at least make sense of it, but I would be wasting my time. And I'd much rather read a good book.

Before I know it, I am half way through the book and there is only five minutes before gym. Dang, time flies when you are deep in a book. I pack up my things and look out the library windows to wait for the bell.

Being in the library allows you to see half the school. It sits in the middle of the building and is two floors tall, the rest of the school circles the library. It is also lined with windows top to bottom. The second floor is the computer lab now, it hadn't always been. I have always thought the library was really something amazing.

The best seats are downstairs next to the office at the front of the school which is also lined with windows from one end of the hall to the other. I look out the windows to see what is going on in the office. People are walking in and out, bustling about, then everyone stops and looks down the hall inside of the office. Well, that is curious. I look out the window in the same direction down towards the guidance counselor's office to see what all of the fuss is about. Hopefully, whatever had everyone else stop and look, will walk out to the hall.

Then something I never thought possible happened. Never before in my life, at Spencer-Van Etten High School, have I seen a more gorgeous guy walk through those office doors. He walks out of the guidance counselor's office at the opposite end of the hall from me and my prayers are answered when he turns my way and starts up the hall.

Mrs. Cross, the guidance counselor, who is about 50 years old, but looks good for 50, is all but drooling and looking ashamed for it. She is also very happily married. Who could blame her though, I am drooling too. Of course, when they get up close to my window, he looks at me. Instead of looking away or at least wiping the drool from my face, I freeze. Nice, Serena, nice.

I can't look away, can't move, can't even breathe. But then neither does he. He keeps walking but never takes his eyes off me. They are the most miraculous eyes I have ever seen too. Bright blue that seem to glow and sparkle, and I swear to you they swirl. And I thought Sam and my dad's eyes were beautiful, they will now look dull. This guy has ruined blue eyes for me forever. I can't look away from those eyes, which is the reason, I am telling myself, for why I am gaping at him; correction, *still* gaping at him.

It seemed like we stared at each other forever and he must have stopped walking because the next thing I know, the bell is ringing and the staring contest ends, Mrs. Cross is pulling him away and he's gone.

I sit there for longer than I should, trying to catch my breath. Shaking my head, I gather my things and go to my locker. I hurry as I collect everything I am going to need to take home, that way I can head straight for Sam's car and don't have to come back up here. And what do you know, I did forget my clothes. Great.

Chapter 2

My 18th birthday started out with my parents going crazy. Then with me bored out of my mind with way too much free time. And then with me leaving my first day of senior year smelly and sweaty because for the first time in 4 years, Mr. Gold decided to have us run the mile the first day of school. REALLY?!

Sam beats me to the car, she must have really moved. She is all but jumping out of her shoes when I get to her.

Sam grabs my arm and drags me to the back of the car to look at none other than *him*. He is leaning on the trunk of his car in the back of the lot with his ankles crossed and looking around as if he is looking for someone. He acts as if he does not even know or care that everyone in a 500-foot radius is checking him out. Yeah, it is that bad and he is that hot, even the guys are looking at him. Okay, maybe they are more glaring at him, but still.

They don't make them like him anymore. He has to be 6 feet tall, lean with muscles ripping over his body. But the good kind that is clearly there but not taking over, you know? The higher up my eyes travel, the more drool builds up; good lord, what is my problem today? He clearly has abs you could wash clothes on, and arms that could easily pick up a 50-pound sack of potatoes, I laugh at the analogy (I'm a country girl, okay).

I give my head a mental shake. I really need to get out more; I am beginning to talk to the voices in my head. Oh no, I have voices in my head, what am I doing? There is easily the hottest man, and yes, he is most *definitely* a man, standing in front of me, and I am worrying about the voices in my head? I can worry about them later.

I turn my attention back to him, I have my priorities straight. I look at his face to see long lashes, which every girl staring at him are undoubtedly jealous of, around those amazing eyes. What I didn't have time to notice earlier is his strong nose, high cheek bones, and full soft lips. Oh, what it would be like to kiss those lips...wow, where did that come from?

Sam still has the grip on my arm that she now uses to pull me out of my hot guy trance. "Serena!?"

"What?" I answer, shaking my head and turning to her, but not actually taking my eyes from him. "Sorry, Sam, did you say something?" I ask looking away, with some effort, from *him*.

Sam laughs, "Yeah, I said a lot of somethings actually, but the important something was if you know who he is? All I have heard is that he might be transferring here but he wanted a tour first." Sam can be a gossip so she knows a lot about a lot of people.

"Oh, well, no, I don't know." Sam looks him over with hungry eyes one more time and I have the pleasure of experiencing a surge of jealousy which surprises me to no end. I stamp down on that and ignore the why.

"Why would he want to do that?" I asked, fighting the urge to look at him again instead taking my arm from Sam and walking to the passenger side of her car.

"What? Transfer here? I don't have a clue," Sam says sliding into the car.

"No, why would he take a tour first? Unless his parents are divorced and one lives in the district," I muse. Sam doesn't turn on the car but instead sits there thinking. I am just about to ask her if she planned on starting the car so we could go when she perks up and looks at me grabbing the door handle. Oh no.

"I don't know. How about we go ask?" Crap, that is what I was afraid of. Sam jumps out of the car before I can say anything. Oh no, oh no, oh no.

"Sam!" I jump out after her and catch her at the trunk of the car next to us. "No, Sam, we can find out tomorrow, you know, ask around. Besides, I should get home. You know, my birthday, I need to go see my parents. I am sure they have some sort of surprise for me." I am babbling, I know, but I am desperate. I can't explain it, but I just know that I can't go near him right now. Besides I really don't need Hotty McHotness to see me drool on myself, or to smell me, I am reminded as the wind shifts.

"Oh, right, sorry, hun! Of course, let's go." Thank goodness for Sam, she knows that there is another reason. I can see it in her bright but now dull eyes, but she doesn't push it. Sam turns and walks to the car but as I am about to follow her, he catches my eye. He had been watching us. Watching me, I realize as I become aware of the tingling going up my spine. Before I can get trapped in his hypnotic eyes, I turn and run to Sam's car, jumping in as she starts it.

Sam talked the whole ride home again, this time I try to be a part of the conversation. Even though it is all about *him*. What is his story? And how gorgeous do two people have to be to create such a…well, there is no word. And now I am vain, great.

Sam pulls into my driveway and puts the car in park. Turning to me she says, "Okay, as part of my present to you, I am going to spend all night calling everyone to find out about the Greek God that showed himself in our school today." I laugh as I grab my bag and get out. I open the back door to be attacked by the balloons and struggle to get them under control. When I finally do and close the door, Sam rolls down the window and leans over, "I will call you with any new information."

"Okay, but remember to do your homework too," I laugh knowing she will get up at the crack of dawn to rush around and do it.

"'Kay, Mom!!" she laughs at me. Sam always says I am like a second mother to her sometimes and it has become a joke with us. "HAPPY BIRTHDAY!!" she yells one last time as she backs out the driveway.

I take my time walking to the house, looking around. My house is a quaint little ranch-style home. Big enough that we aren't on top of each other but small enough that when my dad needs toilet paper, we can hear him, or my mom can hear him; we are close, but I *am not* going there. I look over to the big oak tree in my front yard thinking of all the times my mom and I used to climb it. I get a strange urge to climb it now but the balloons in my hands stop me. Instead, I walk to the front door. I only get one step on the porch when I feel like someone is watching me. Turning

19

around I look up and down the road. My spine tingles and I shake my head.

I continue to the door, but before I can open it, my mom is there. "Good, you're home, come sit down, we need to talk," she says grabbing my arm and dragging me in. She doesn't even give me a chance to set down my stuff, instead pushes me toward the couch across from my dad who is in the chair, then shoves me down on it.

They both look nervous, which just makes me more nervous. "About what we told you this morning," my mom starts and I tense, not this again. I really hoped we could just forget about that. Apparently not.

"Guys, the joke is over, you got me. Now if you don't mind, I really want to relax, it has been a long day," I say, turning to find the remote.

"Honey, we are not kidding around. You are a witch and you need to understand this," my dad says, looking to my mom to explain. I look to her too, hoping to see the quick smile that is always there. But it isn't now, all I see is sadness and regret, not a good sign.

Then my mom looks to the bowl of M&M's on the coffee table and, right before my eyes, it floats in the air. No, there must be a reason; I stand up and wave my arms all around, looking for the string. My jaw drops to the floor.

"Seri, honey, this is no joke, you are a witch. Our powers lay dormant until our 18th birthday. There is so much I need to tell you; to explain to you...." I interrupt her, not being able to take it.

"The first had better be why you didn't tell me before. Why you allowed me to think I could have a normal life!?" I didn't start out yelling but by the end, I was. I already know the answer though, so my anger deflates somewhat after the outburst. My parents have always wanted the best for me and have always wanted me to enjoy life. This kind of information would have changed everything. I am a bit of a worrier; I would have spent my life until now fretting about the powers that would awaken. That is no way to live.

The M&M's drop back to the table. "Yes, Serena, that is why." My mind blanks with that statement. Oh Lord, I was right to worry this morning about her saying what I didn't say out loud. Am I making any sense? That didn't sound right in my head. Maybe *I* am the one going crazy! "Serena, you are not going crazy, I am sorry, I will stay out of your head." I fall back to the couch. She is in my head, or was, I… oh god.

What has my mom heard me think all these years?! My parents and I are close but I don't tell them everything! Oh no, does she know that I kissed Jack Owen in the 5th grade? Or that I snuck out to meet Sam last April to go to a club? Oh my… does she know that… "Serena, calm down, I have only started reading your mind, to gauge how you are taking all this. I respect your privacy." Oh, thank the Goddess!

I look to my dad with a question, one that he guesses at or reads my mind to find out. "No, Seri, just you and your mom." Okay, so my dad is normal, lucky him. Figures that this is what my senior year would come to. My mother being able to know everything; so much for a fun and crazy last year. Not that that is what it was going to be like anyway. Dang, I really need to learn to have more fun.

Okay, Serena, that is not the biggest problem here! You are a witch! I wonder if witches have more fun, like blondes. Okay, get back on track, Serena Rae.

Chapter 3

"You know, just because I love those teen paranormal books doesn't mean I want to be a part of one," I say before muttering to myself, "All that is missing is the hunky hero." The next thing I know, my mom is muttering something that I really do not want to hear.

"For now, anyway."

"Excuse me? What the—"

"Language!" my dad interrupts.

"—heck, does that mean?" I ask, not really wanting to know the answer. I have a very bad feeling that it is something I am not going to be happy about. "I don't plan on dating anyone this year. I need to concentrate on my GPA and finding a job and college applications. I don't even know where I am going next year. Besides, any relationship I have this year will have to end when I go to college. What would be the point?" I say, and my dad looks very happy at that. A second later, he gets this beaten look on his handsome face that crushes what little hope I had of being right.

"You don't have a choice, Serena."

"What!?! I am not going to be set up by my parents!"

"Not us, you know your father would rather see you single till you're 30."

"You know that's right!" I have to laugh, my dad always ends up sounding like Gus from *Psych*.

"Okay, how about I start at the beginning?" And with my nod, she starts. I am ready to finish this horror story and go to bed. "Alright, you have learned a little about the witch hunts in school, right?" I shake my head as I laugh, yeah, figures it would start there. When she doesn't continue, I nod.

"You know what," she says looking to my father, then back at me, "perhaps I should start in the middle so you don't freak out." That is reassuring, I lean back on the couch and tuck my feet under me. Now I am ready for the horror movie to continue. "Okay, witches are not the only supernatural beings out there. Vampires, werewolves, and so on are all real." She pauses, waiting to see if I have a question. I am just not surprised, I am sure the Boogieman and Tooth Fairy are real. Nothing would surprise me at this point.

"Go on," I say when she continues to wait for my freak-out.

"Not all of them live here of course, most live on a separate plane. Do you know what that means?" she asks and I nod. My parents are pagans, not sure what I believe. They raised me to think for myself and I just never thought about my beliefs, not yet anyway. I have a feeling that is about to change too. With them being pagan though, I know about the different planes, realms, dimensions, or whatever you want to call them. Pagans believe in these different worlds. We live in one and other beings (including the dead) live in others. When the veil between these worlds is thin, they can cross over.

"Well, all of these beings use witches to keep them hidden. The ones that are well known live on this plane with us. You know, vampires and all kinds of shifters, they use us the most. They would also, on occasion, need a random spell. This made the witches very rich. The witch hunts were started by the church because they coveted our wealth and standing with the people. This caused us to go into hiding, to act as normal as possible, meaning no more magic. Then something changed. They started to find and burn real witches. No one knew how this was. Most casted one more spell, this spell caused the hunters to look another way."

"Well, that is just cruel. Innocent people died instead," I say, a bit disgusted.

"You are right, and the families felt horrible for that, but you must understand it was for the greater good. Without witches, the humans would soon learn that the monsters in the night are real and start a new hunt. If they started to hunt the paranormal beings, well, take how many innocents died during the witch hunts and put in the number that survived in its place. Humans would go crazy and just start killing each other out of fear. The world would kill itself off trying to kill a few."

"Okay, I get it, but still." She pauses for a moment looking sorry.

"Anyway, it didn't make any since that the hunters were finding and killing real witches."

"Why wouldn't the witches use their magic to send them away, or better yet, protect themselves?" I ask, getting a little into the story despite myself.

"Good question. We don't use our magic to harm others. Wait...before you interrupt to say the spell did harm others..." She is right, I was going to say that. "The spell was a look-not-this-way spell. It did not harm. That was the hunters." I guess she is right. The spell just caused the hunters not to look to them, it did not make them go to others.

"So why would it not work suddenly? And, why not cast it again?"

"When the families found out that a witch family was killed, they did cast it again but it was not working. Then they found out why. A family that was being taken was able to get one last spell cast, one that informed the others what had gone wrong. The hunters had an amulet on. This amulet protected them from being spelled or having any spell affect them. The good thing though, the amulet also told us who had turned the witches over to be killed. The Birch family, they are a family of witches who are greedy and conniving. All they care about is power and money. Luckily, it was centered in the big cities. So, the families on the outskirts were safe. Unfortunately, our family lived in London and just happened to be one of the most powerful families."

"So how did our family survive?" I had to interrupt to ask.

"The Birch family personally told the hunters where to find us because we were so powerful. They didn't expect one thing though," my mom turns to my dad.

"They had Dad?" I ask, trying not to laugh.

25

"No," my mom laughs. "Your great grandmother had her soul mate. That is a very rare and very powerful thing. You see, honey, we are but one half of a whole person. Your power...well, it grows to your full potential when you are with your soul mate. That is why the spell worked. Her magic was more powerful than the Birch family's amulet." She had grabbed my dad's hand during that explanation.

"So, to protect future generations, she cast a spell. This spell was so powerful that it killed them both."

"What was the spell?" I ask, officially enthralled.

"The spell was to ensure that future generations found their soul mates. I thank them both every day. That spell led your father to me, it gave me you. You are 18 now. Your power has been awakened, that means that the spell is in play, your soul mate will find you. No matter where he is, or what he is doing, he will come." That caught my *full* undivided attention.

I stutter...I spew...I don't even know where to start. "What!? When?! What!? No, this can't be happening. What happened to my year of me? Concentrating on school and getting into college, my future. Seeing the world."

"Yes, honey, by him being with you, you will be more powerful and be able to protect yourself and your future family. You will be whole." She is smiling, why is she smiling? I just found out that my entire life is turning upside down with an added twist of a soul mate coming to find me and she is smiling like it's a good thing. I am not seeing where the smiles come in!

"I cannot wait for you to experience the feeling of being whole; complete. Don't worry, Serena. The moment you see him, you will be instantly drawn to him. Looking into

26

his eyes for even a second will feel like a lifetime, and it will still not be long enough. He will be the most attractive man you have ever and will ever see." Oh no, this is all starting to sound familiar. "When you aren't near him, you feel as though a piece of you is missing. All you want is to run to him." Oh, my… no, no, no, no, no, no.

He showed up out of nowhere – check.

I could swim in his eyes for eternity – check.

I will admit, only to myself, this one time, that since leaving that parking lot, I have felt a very strong need to go back to him – check.

Even my inner monologue's voice is starting to sound high-pitched and panicked!

If what my mom is saying is true, then HE is my soul mate and I am so not ready for this!

I get up from the couch ready to run when my mom grabs my arm, "Wait, Serena…"

"Mom, I need to be alone and think."

"I know. I just need you to understand. You cannot tell anyone about this. And we will start tomorrow."

"Start what tomorrow?"

"Practice. Your powers have awakened, Serena, you need to learn how to use and control them. The Others will have sensed a new witch and they may come to you for help. You need to practice. More than that, the Birch family is still around, they have been quiet since the failure of the witch trials, but if they sense weakness, that may change." She says all this as if it should have all accrued to me but all I can think about is *him*.

"The Others, Mom? Do we really need to be that ominous?" I say. Really, it just needed to be asked.

"Well, it is easier than listing them all out, Serena. There is a lot of them."

Great, just what I need in my senior year, a list of supernatural beings coming to me for help!

Chapter 4

I can't sleep. Who could blame me though? My entire life just got flipped upside down and my parents are acting like everything is fine and dandy, nothing has changed. But everything has changed, for me. Everything just keeps spinning around in my head. All that I learned. All that may be coming. I am getting such a headache! I don't need all this. I didn't ask for it, but I guess I have no choice.

I sit up in bed and lean my head on the headboard, while looking around my room. The sage walls, the dream catcher over my bed. All the pictures, mostly of my parents and Sam. Jeez, I need to get a life. That thought seems to be a reoccurring one.

Looking around, it would seem my life, me, that it was all the same as yesterday, but it is all about to change. Has changed.

Alright, time to put my big girl panties on and suck it up. I throw myself back on the pillow and scream. Okay, now I am done. No more feeling sorry for myself. Tomorrow is a new day and I am going to smile and make the best of it. I cuddle deep into my mattress and take a deep breath before falling asleep.

I wake up the next morning more tired than when I went to sleep. I kept having a dream about being on fire and not being scared because I was looking into *his* eyes. I wonder if witches can make fire climb up their arms like in my dream. I sit up in bed rubbing the last of sleep out of my eyes. I look around my room and scream, jumping out of my bed. My parents come running into my room only to crash into me, nearly throwing me on the floor. The only thing that saved me from going down is the fact that I am a stone statue staring at my bed, and my dad may have caught me, I can't be sure.

The only thing that has my full attention is my scorched bed. Burnt sheets and all. So are my pajamas, but I'm fine. How am I fine? I look to my mom who is staring at the bed with a big smile. Again with the smile!

"Are you okay, Serena?" my dad asks, snapping out of the zoned-out scared look and turning me around, looking for burns.

"I'm fine, what happened?" I ask my mom.

"Oh, Seri, this is amazing! You created fire! That is your element. I cannot believe you were able to create it your first night! That never happens! You are going to be powerful indeed! I wonder what will manifest when he comes." I am not sure that is a good thing. I am about to freak out. BREATHE, SERENA! My mind is yelling at me.

"Okay, well, I don't have time to have a panic attack, I need to get to school," I say, grabbing my clothes out of my closet and heading to the bathroom. I spend a little more time in the shower than I usually would, but I think I deserve that little luxury.

I meet Sam outside and act like everything is normal, because it is, dammit! The ride to school is again one-sided but I do pay attention and not because of the subject. *Not* because of the subject.

"Okay, so I wasn't able to find out a whole lot which is why I didn't call you last night." I. Am. An. Ass. I did not even realize that she never called.

"It's okay, Sam, I was really busy last night with my parents anyway. So, what did you learn?" I don't care. I don't care. I don't care. I know the more I repeat it, it doesn't make it true. Don't judge me.

"Well, no one really knows anything. He came in, talked to Mrs. Cross, got a tour, and left. But Sandy said that she was in the office when he came in and overheard that his name is Damian, and that he is from Ithaca," I laugh, Sam sounds so disappointed.

"That is, well, not a whole lot but it is okay, Sam, we can find out more, don't worry."

Sam gives me the stink eye as she parks the car. "It is a lot safer if you look straight ahead while you drive, but it is even more so while parking."

That just got me a stinkier stink eye. "I don't care about not getting a lot of info on him. For how hot he is, it is not possible he came from Ithaca, NY! Why can't he be from Italy, or France, or somewhere we can't drive to in a half an hour!! Dammit, I wanted to travel in order to meet his family and have our wedding abroad!" I laugh again, even though the thought of Sam marrying him makes me want to kill her. That is not okay!

"Well, you will meet your foreign hotty someday, I promise," I tell her when we met at the front of the car and start toward the school. I am about to tell her that I will help her find him so I can go to the wedding in Italy when I notice that everyone is looking to the parking lot. I turn around with Sam and my mouth hits the pavement. Damian is back, and from the looks of it, for good.

He is still leaning against his car just as I left him yesterday, but today he has a back pack. He is wearing jeans and a black shirt that clings to his chest. I cannot believe that I am jealous, of a shirt. New low. I force my eyes away from his chest and notice that he has a *really* nice car. I was so busy ogling him yesterday *Insert not being creepy here…please* that I didn't notice it.

Most kids here have Junker cars and trucks, and some even drive tractors and 4-wheelers to school. Not Mister Sexy though. He drives a new Porsche Panamera. No doubt about it now, he is *definitely* from Ithaca, NY. Must be nice to have a new car, hell, it must be nice to have *a* car. Hey, I wonder if I can conjure a car with my new powers.

I start laughing as I turn away walking to the school. Sam catches up to me as I get to the side walk. "What is so funny?" she asks.

"Nothing, just how everyone is reacting to Damian," I lie. Well, I kind of lied; it is funny but not at all surprising. It is not often we get fresh meat and never one as tasty as him. Really? Did I just seriously think that!? What is my problem lately? I don't want this, don't need this. I have plans, dreams… kind of. Okay, so really the only thing is to move and figure out what I want to do with my life. But still, that does not include a guy. Yet.

"Excuse me?" Oh. My. God… that voice. It's like chocolate, smooth, and oh-so-sweet. Dammit, why do I have to love chocolate? Without even turning around, I know who is behind me. Without ever hearing that voice, I know it. I have known that voice all my life.

No, I know who is behind me because I had been ignoring his approach. I felt every step he took towards me. I felt it through my entire being. It felt as though I had been stretched out my entire life and was just now feeling it, just now noticing it, because I was finally coming back to myself. I am right, Damian is my soul mate, and I am absolutely terrified to turn around. I know that if I do, there is no turning back and I am just not ready for this.

I am getting ready to run when he puts his hand on my shoulder and just like that the earth shakes. It literally shakes; more than likely it is just me, just my world. I turn around, too shocked not to. Too caught up in the weightlessness of his touch. The fire in his touch.

SNAP. The moment I turn and look into his eyes, it is like a rubber band snapping back into place. In that moment, I know what it feels like to really breathe. One touch and one look from the right person and I can fly.

This feeling is something that few feel and that takes me a second to get used to. I can't move, can't think. Just feel. This is what I was afraid of, why I wanted to avoid him. I feel as though for the first time I know who I am meant to be and who I am meant to be with. I know without a doubt that though I do not know him, I would die without him. Damn!

"What just happened?" Damian asks without removing his hand from my shoulder. He is staring at his hand as if it is new and he isn't sure why he can't move it. Well, I understand because I didn't want him to move it. Dammit.

33

I really need to learn control, at least over my own thoughts and feelings. I'm screwed.

"Um, hi, I'm Serena. You're Damian, right?" I say with a 'don't worry, all will be alright as soon as I know what just happened' smile. I hope.

"Yes, I'm Damian, I was just wondering if you can tell me how to get to Accounting?" Of course he is in Accounting with me. It would be my luck that the first thing he learns about me is how horrible I am at math. 1+1=2, that is how far my knowledge goes with math.

And like the wonderful friend that I am, I had completely forgotten Sam until she speaks up, "Of course Seri can. That is her first class too." Oh, I hadn't spoken yet. Stupid, but how can I when he hasn't stopped staring into my eyes, trapping me and my brain functions.

"Oh yeah," I say, giving my head a shake. I turn and start to the school. He takes his hand off my shoulder as I start walking but he doesn't stop touching me. He lets his hand slide down my arm but keeps his fingers on mine. Great, my life has gone from a horror movie to those teen romance movies that make me gag, and I am not helping it any. Every time our bodies drift apart, my hand goes out to keep the contact and so does his. That is how it went until we reached the lockers and went our separate ways.

I put my things away and grab my accounting notebook. When I close my locker, instead of heading to Sam, like I normally would have, I turn to Damian, while Sam gives me that knowing smile the whole time. She waves bye and heads to class. I can't help it though. With him just coming near me, I felt the pull, but that touch made it a frickin' anchor that I do not have the power to break, even with my voice for freedom and free-will screaming at me in the back of my head. I just don't want to break it anymore, five minutes of this and I love the feeling of being whole too much to want to break it. I can't even explain what it feels like, not even to myself. Just…wow. It feels as if I am breathing for the first time. Seeing for the first time. Truly feeling for the first time.

His eyes are addicting, I realize as he closes his locker and looks down the hall at me, nearly knocking me off my feet. I force myself not to run to him. I remind myself that I just met him, literally five minute ago. I can't run up to him and jump into his arms.

Besides, I sense something about him. It's nagging at me. Damn this came on fast.

Damian's hand twitches, causing me to look down. He has his hand in a fist and he is stiff, holding himself completely still. I guess he is forcing himself not to run to me too. Good, not just me then.

"You ready?" I ask, coming to a stop in front of him, and trying to sound as casual as possible.

"After you," he says with a slight bow. I laugh at the old gesture and start to walk, allowing him to fall into step beside me. *I don't want him to touch me. I don't want him to touch me. I don't want him to touch me.*

"So, what made you decide to transfer? The cows you can see out of every window?" I ask. Damian chuckles, but after a couple steps he hadn't answered. "I'm sorry, it's none of my business," I say, stopping to look up at him. He's staring at me, has been since we started walking, "What? Is there something on my face?" Oh, just shoot me now.

"No, you're perfect," he says in the most sincere tone I have ever heard. I feel the blood rush to my cheeks. "To be honest, you are the reason I transferred. I wasn't really sure why I was here yesterday, but when I saw you sitting in the library, I didn't care why anymore." The warning bell rings but neither off us moves.

He had stayed for me. That is either really creepy or really romantic, and right now looking into his swirling blue eyes, I am going with romantic. I am choosing to ignore that it might have had more to do with the spell than with me. A girl has to have something, right?

"Are you always this straight-forward and honest?" I ask, liking that he had been. I hate games. Maybe he *is* perfect for me. How had I gone from not wanting this to don't ever leave me so fast? Oh right, the eyes. And the smile. And the abs, damn I'm shallow. This attraction, this pull, is strong. Stronger than I thought it would be.

He smiles at me. "I don't like games, and since I am being honest," he steps closer to me and leans down so his lips are right next to my ear, and I stop breathing, "I know you are a witch and you should know that I'm a vampire." He leans back to stare deep into my eyes. His eyes have gone from complete confusion over what is happening with us, and slight adoration, to fear and worry.

Why would he be afraid? I am the one who, just last night, found out that I am a witch. And because that isn't enough, the universe felt the need to send me a vampire as my soul mate. I cannot believe that thought just went through my head. Where has my life gone?

Suddenly, I become aware of a burning in my lungs. Slowly it moves up through my throat. Why can't I breathe?

What is happening? Oh my god, I'm dying! I am too young to have a heart attack! How had this day gone from bad, to interesting, to worse, and it isn't even 8:15 in the morning!?

"Breathe, Serena, breathe." He has a hold on my shoulders, books forgotten on the floor, looking right into my eyes not breaking my gaze. I can feel his calm. His steady breathing comes into me, washes over me. Before I can completely calm, he turns his head, next thing I know we are in the weight room. The door had been right behind us, we hadn't gotten very far in our walk. Wait…

"How?" that is all I got out before I couldn't breathe again.

"Serena, breathe, you are having a panic attack, you just need to breathe." His hands are back on my shoulders massaging. That calms me in no time allowing me to take deep breathes again. I never have panic attacks so this is a new experience for me.

"You are a witch, how do you not know about vampires? Or is it the rule that is freaking you out? Wait, never mind, you wouldn't know about that," he whispers that last part which snaps me out of it.

"Rule? What rule? I just found out last night that I am a witch and only because my powers awakened. My parents told me that other things are out there but I hadn't met any yet, that I know of anyways. I sure as hell was not expecting to have my soul mate be…"

"Wait, what do you mean soul mate? Is that why this feels so strong so fast?" He looks as though he is about to have a panic attack and I have a strong urge to comfort him.

I take a deep breath in through my nose and his scent calms me. "Okay, it would seem that we both have some explaining to do. You go first," I tell him. I need to think about how I am going to explain the whole soul mate thing.

"Well...um...I guess I'll start at the beginning." He is quiet for a minute, collecting his thoughts. "What did your parents tell you?" I laugh. He looks so lost and so cute.

"Okay, I'll go first," I say, coming to his rescue and he visibly lets out a breath. I can't help but smile. This, us, feels so natural.

I'm quiet for a minute, trying to figure out what I should tell him. He doesn't rush me. Instead, Damian goes over to the wrestling mat in the corner and sits. I follow slowly to give myself more time. I sit next to him and he reaches out his hand to take mine.

"Sorry, I can't help it," he says looking sheepish. I smile at him not sure what to say. I feel the need to have contact with him to. It does feel natural and nice to be near him, but my independent self is still screaming. I think I will just have to ignore it or overpower it with Damian's voice. That works too. I smile at him for real this time and his return smile makes my knees melt. Good thing I am sitting down. I look away and give my head a shake, I need to focus.

"Um...okay...well, my parents told me that I am a witch just yesterday. It was my 18th birthday so my powers awakened."

"Happy birthday," he stops me to say.

"Thanks. I guess my family is one of the most powerful."

"What is your last name?" Damian interrupts me again to ask.

"Rae."

His eyes pop just a little. "Yes, you are most certainly the most powerful family." I think he wanted to know. I think he confirmed it because he had heard the doubt in my voice. I just found all this out, how would I know for sure how powerful we are?

"Well, I guess the story would start during the witch hunts. Another family, the Birch family, wanted to kill my ancestors to help them gain more power and used the hunters to do that. The hunters wore an amulet that made spells not affect them, but my family's spell did work. My grandmother, I really don't know how many greats so let's stick with just grandmother, had her soul mate. Being with him made her whole and therefore more powerful than the Birch family." I stop and look to Damian to make sure that he understood that. When he nods, I continue, "Okay, so in the hopes of protecting future generations, my grandmother along with the help of her soul mate, my grandfather, cast one last spell. Basically, on the 18th birthday, when our powers awaken, our soul mates, no matter where they are or what they are doing, will come to us. Hence you being here, and the strong feelings and pull to be near each other and to have contact," I say looking into his eyes and squeezing his hand holding mine.

He is silent for a moment and just when I start to get nervous, he squeezes my hand and looks at me. "This is not going to be easy. First, there is more to that story not many know about it."

"Wait…there is? How do you know that?"

"I…" When I think about my parents sitting me down and telling me even more about that story, I want to run. Damian, well, I could listen to him talk about physics and be enthralled. His voice is like chocolate silk running through my bones. I must be staring at him because he smiles at me. "I don't know what you are thinking but you look adorable thinking it." He turns away and shakes his head. "Okay, the witch hunts were started by the church but Melinda Birch saw it as an opportunity to take control. Honestly though, I don't think she would have if it wasn't for William, but this is a story that I should tell you with your parents." That got me out of the smile-induced fog. I look at him shocked.

"Why? What? Why? You want to meet my parents? We just met! Why?" His smile at my near panicked voice had me melting into a puddle. Jeez, I am turning into a girly girl. Well really, that *is* better than panic attacks.

"Yes, Serena. I don't want to tell it twice and they should know that I am here and moreover, that I am a vampire," Damian says laughing and pulling me up so we can start to the door. When we reach the door, he leans his ear up to it, "Can you text Sam and let her know that we are leaving?"

"Now?" I squeal. Damian looks back at me with a smile in his eyes.

"Would you rather stay here all day and fret about bringing me home later?" he asks laughing. Damn him, he is right, it would drive myself crazy.

"Fine," I say pulling out my phone and texting Sam. He's listening at the door but his eyes are on me. "What?" I ask.

"You are so cute. Your parents knew I was coming but you are so nervous to introduce me. Is it because I'm a vampire?" he asks, more as an afterthought. I guess that thought makes him a bit nervous because it took the smile out of his eyes. He is worried and maybe even a little scared to meet them, I can see that. But the thought of me not liking that he is a vampire, that actually scares him.

My being scared about his being a vampire would make more sense, but though they are not going to be thrilled by that, my parents will understand that there is nothing they can do. No, it is just the fact of bringing a boy home. It is something I have never done.

Chapter 5

I feel him looking at me, waiting. When I look up, it is to see that Damian isn't listening at the door anymore but staring down at me, looking more nervous by the second. Damn he's tall. "No," I say squeezing his hand, "no, it's just that you are the first guy I have, or will, ever bring home. I know that they have been expecting you but just the thought of bringing you home and introducing you to my parents, is a little scary, especially since I just met you," I say with a slightly shy smile.

"Oh, good," he says with relief in his voice though I can tell that something is still bothering him.

"What is it?" I ask. He doesn't answer at first, just looks at me.

Finally, he takes a deep breath. "How *do* you feel about me being a vampire? How do you feel about us being soul mates actually?" he asks. I wasn't expecting that so I laugh a little, which has his nervous look coming back; okay, so it was a slightly manic sounding laugh. He really shouldn't have that look though, it is just not him. I grab both of his hands and squeeze, making sure he is looking into my eyes.

"I was shocked and not at all happy last night when my parents told me about being a witch. I was even less happy about the soul mate thing," he starts to get a defeated look in his eyes, which makes me smile.

Mean, I know, but seeing that my not liking the idea bothers him is reassuring. "Then I *met* my soul mate and though I am still not happy about my plans for my future changing, I am happy that I met my other half. Which is a surprise because I didn't think I would be. As for you being a vampire, well, I think that helps with all this. You understand and can relate to my being different because you are too. You can also help me adjust to this new world. I didn't even realize that till now." He had started smiling and now that smile reaches his eyes. "How do you feel about all this? At least I had noticed you were literally torn away from everything and dragged to the middle of nowhere to have me plopped in your life," I say.

He releases one of my hands and places his on the side of my face, brushing it lightly into my hair, greatly distracting me and causing me to inadvertently lean my head into his palms. It's all warm and smooth. Rubbing his thumb along my cheek he says simply, "I have lived alone long enough." I hear the smile in his voice, with my eyes closed I can't see it. With him rubbing his thumb up and down my jaw, I can't muster the strength to open my eyes to see his smile. Besides, I am already weak because of what he is doing, add his smile to that and I would probably faint. Wouldn't that be attractive?

"Serena?" Damian says laughing, and I finally open my eyes. I had felt the heat radiating off him telling me he had stepped closer, but now he is so close only air could slide between us. I grab hold of his shirt at his sides to help hold myself up and I look up into his eyes. Luckily, he has stopped with the thumb rubbing thing so I am able to stay on my feet.

"My god, your eyes are beautiful," he whispers and I stop breathing. "Um...I don't remember what I was going to say," he says, letting out a nervous laugh. He drops his hands and steps away from me. It must have been the look on my face that makes him regret the action immediately, because he comes right back to where he had left saying, "No, Serena, I'm sorry but we can't stay in here, we need to go and being this close to you makes me forget myself. All I can think about is kissing you."

I laugh. "I'm okay with that," I say before I can stop myself. Damian closes his eyes and places his forehead on mine.

With a smile he says, "Don't say things like that. As much as I would love that, we really do need to go and I know that as soon as I kiss you, I will never want to stop." He opens his eyes and looks deep into mine. "Come on, everyone is in class, we need to go now," he says but doesn't move just keeps staring into my eyes. Then his eyes begin to travel down to my lips. I know that I need to step back to stop what he is thinking, and damn me, but I just don't want to stop him.

Thirty minutes of knowing him and already all I want is to be in his arms and never leave. Crap, he is right, the moment our lips touch, neither of us will have the control to stop. We just met, we need to get to know each other, and of course the people that will be clogging the halls, that is important too, but I can't seem to remember why. I step back before I lose the ability to do so. Damian drops his hands and takes a deep breath. "Thank you."

I laugh. "Don't ever expect me to be able to do that again." Damian looks at me. His eyes travel down to my toes and slowly back up. I feel every spot his eyes take in. "Stop. You are messing with my equilibrium." I laugh out breathlessly.

"Sorry," he says, just as breathless. "It's the first time I have really gotten a look at you." Turning around, he leans back into the door and listens. "By the way," he says as a passing thought, looking at me out of the corner of his eyes, "you are stronger than you think." He comes over to me and grabs my hand, rushing us out of the door and down the stairs.

Before I can even register what is happening, we are in his car. The really nice brand-new Porsche; damn Porsches. The sad part is that this is the only time I have ever been in a car newer than 2005, which is what my parents drive, a '05 Jeep Liberty.

My mind works in weird ways because with that thought I remember a very important question. "How old are you?" I ask as he pulls out of the parking lot. Damian looks over at me, then back to the road flexing his hand on the stirring wheel. That is when I notice that we are still holding hands. It feels so normal that I hadn't even noticed, I can't help but smile. "Well, you said you have lived long enough alone so I was just wondering how long that would be," I say trying to make the question a little less...I don't know, heavy, I guess.

"You have the right to ask so don't feel bad for asking. I just don't want you to freak out," he says looking at me again, smiling crookedly. And here I thought he couldn't get any cuter. "Okay," he takes a deep breath before he begins, "I was born in 1530 and I was turned in 1549, so I am...464. Sorry, I haven't celebrated my birthday in a while." He keeps his attention on me even though he turns back to the road. I school my features.

So... he is old. Most girls want to date older guys, thought I feel like four hundred and sixty-four may be pushing the older guys' obsession, right? But he looks damn good for 464, and there is my vain side again.

Okay, he was 19 when he was turned, I secretly figure out on my fingers. Ugh, I am pathetic. That is how I will look at it. "So, 19 huh?" I say. Damian turns off the car and looks at me, pure relief in his beautiful eyes.

"Yeah, 19," he laughs. Wait, he turned the car off, I look around to see that we are in my driveway. How the... I look back at him to see that he is looking down at our joined hands. "I followed you and Sam yesterday. I didn't know why at the time, I just had to." He looks up at me. His eyes looked sad and scared.

"I understand why. It took everything I had not to make Sam turn back yesterday. If it hadn't been for her in the car talking and distracting me, I would have never left that parking lot."

Laughing, he gets out of the car and in the next instant is at my door pulling it open.

"We don't have to worry about my parents not being home, my family owns a farmstand so they work from home. My mom does more of the gardening, though we all pitch in, and my dad takes care of the stand and finances," I tell him as we start to walk up the driveway. "It's September, so they will be in the greenhouses," I say as Damian starts toward the house but with my hand that is

46

once again in his, I pull him to the side of the house. He gives me a questioning look. "They will be in the greenhouses out back," I tell him in answer.

We don't start to walk around though because he is dead weight on my hand. "What?" I ask.

"Your heart his beating really fast. You are so nervous," he answers. So as not to let go of my hand, he raises his other to my chin and forces me to peer into his eyes. "It'll be okay. I promise. We do need to talk to your parents so let's just get this over with, okay?"

"Are you going to ask for my hand?" I joke, trying to get my mind off what is happening. I never thought that I would be nervous bringing a guy home to meet my parents. Maybe it is the whole bringing a vampire home to meet the parents, I tell myself that, but that isn't it either. In reality, I am nervous because he is the last man I will bring home. This is it for me.

"Well, I thought we would get to know each other first but…" he replies in a serious voice, tilting his head as if thinking.

"Wait! I was kidding. I'm not…" then he looks at me and I see the sparkle in his eyes, "not cool," I say shaking my head and swatting at his arm. He laughs as I start walking away, dragging him behind me by our still-joined hands.

"You started it," he laughs and I can't help but laugh with him. His laugh is musical and contagious.

I stop and look at him. "Fine, but you have opened a can of worms you so did not want open. It's on now."

"Is it? Bring it on, witch," he says with a smile and I laugh again. I turn and keep walking. "So your parents own

47

a farmstand, how do you guys do way up here?" We come around the back corner of the house and before I can answer, Damian is once again dead weight on my arm, stopping me. I turn back to see what is wrong only to see him staring in awe at the back yard. I turn and look too. It really is beautiful. "Damn!" he breaths.

"Yeah, we do okay way up here," I laugh. "It started out as just a small greenhouse for us but we enjoyed gardening as a family so my dad built the second larger one thinking to sell some here and there. Word got out that our food was really good and really cheap. As more people came up here to get some, the more greenhouses we needed. Then we put in the orchards on both side and the kiwi trees behind. The greenhouse that is attached to the house," I turn and point at it, "that is for us. The first one is filled with what we donate to the local homeless shelters and needy families around town. The rest we sell."

"Well, it *is* amazing. You all work in the greenhouses?" he asks looking at me.

"I focus more on the walk to get to them." His eyes turn to saucers and that is when I realize that it was my garden that had made him stop in the first place. I really shouldn't be surprised, you can barely see the greenhouse behind the flower garden to get there. I have always been so proud of the greenhouses that I forget how spectacular the walk to them really is to someone who has never seen it.

"My mom always says that you should never garden while mad, or stressed, or sad," I tell him as we start walking through the flower garden. "You cannot walk through here and come out the other side and not be anything but calm, peaceful, and happy. She says that is why our food is so good," I tell him, beginning for the first time to feel proud of myself, "I made it so that is flows from season to season, looking full all year. Then I placed benches that are covered in ivy throughout. It is my own little oasis and my favorite place. My mom helped with the setup so I can't take full credit."

We are half way through the flower garden, standing under the weeping cherry tree when Damian stops. Using the hand he has in mine, he pulls me to him. He wraps me up in his arms and once again I stop breathing, which really can't be good for me. My nervous system is going to shut down one of these times.

Damian leans down and runs his nose along my neck breathing me in. "You are amazing," he says leaning his forehead against mine again. With his hands now on my lower back, I can't think of anything but the breath on my neck and the feel of his warm hands on my back.

"It gets better. You should see it at night. We put lights all throughout," that is all I can think to say and I said that so breathless, it was no more than a whisper. I can't even be sure how I was able to speak in that moment. My mind is nothing more than mush.

Damian laughs and considers my eyes, and it feels just as it had this morning. Why it does, I have no idea, this isn't the first time we have been this close and looked at each other so intensely.

Maybe because we know each other this time, at least a little. Or maybe because we have both come to realize that whatever force had chosen us to complete the other, is right? I know that I have anyway, and the way that Damian looks at me has me believing he has too. Either way, it is strong.

I realize though that it is a little different this time. It is a need to be close to him, to never have his touch leave me. It is a need to feel his lips on mine always. Before I can blink, he is standing behind the bench that sits under the weeping cherry, and I feel cold.

Chapter 6

I know my emotions are written all over my face. So when Damian looks up at me from behind the bench and his beautiful face breaks out with regret, I'm not surprised. "Serena, I'm sorry. I… not yet."

I know what he means, we still only just met and we need to get to know each other. No matter how it feels. Yet, not being near him hurts.

"I understand. I just don't like it when I'm not near you. I don't know how to… do you think in time it won't be so hard to not have your hand in mine?" I ask knowing that I sound needy, and in this moment I feel weak. I do not like that. Less than a day, less than 2 hours, and this is what I am turning into. Great, my worst nightmare come true.

"I'm sure it will and if not, at least we will learn to deal with it. I'm more worried about controlling my need to kiss you until it is appropriate." I laugh at that.

"You do realize it is the 21st century, right?" I ask looking at him as if he had lost his mind as he comes around the bench, walking slowly to me.

"Yes, I do, but you'll have to forgive me. Kissing a girl before courting her, moreover, having intimate relations with a girl the same night you meet her, is a bit of a new concept. So, I will stick with the old guy way."

"The old guy way? Really?" I try to be serious but the goofy smile he has on ruins that idea. I laugh as he reaches me and takes my hand. He slowly and gently caresses it.

"Yes, the old guy way. You know, courting a girl?" He very slowly moves up to nearly be touching my entire body. Looking down into my eyes, he says very softly, "Can I court you, Serena Rae?" I can't breathe again, my knees shake. I don't even register what he says, just the way he says it.

Then he puts that goofy smile on again. Oh, he knows how to work that charm and sense of humor. Damn him. Then I realize what he said and start laughing so hard that my side starts to hurt.

"Next you'll be asking if we can go steady."

"One step at a time," he says as he turns to continue our walk. But I am in hysterics and can barely stand.

Seriously, this guy... amazing. "Okay let's go, I am sure that they already know I am here," I say when I can breathe again.

We continue out of the garden holding hands. When we reach the back gate, my parents come walking out of the first greenhouse. I am not surprised to see them come out of there. That is the greenhouse we use for the donations and it is the one we worry about first. Depending on the need, sometimes even before our own.

My mom of course is not surprised to see me, she has always known when I get home. Now I know how. My dad though looks very surprised to see me, I am supposed to be in school after all. But they are both well, shocked, to see Damian.

"Serena Rae! Why are you with a vampire?"

"What? I just wanted to know why she isn't in school! And holding some guy's hand! A vampire? You said that wouldn't happen yet!" my dad says turning to my mom.

"I didn't think it would, honey, they would have sensed a new witch in the area but would know she is new and can't help them yet," my mom answered trying to calm my dad down. He then turns to Damian not at all happy about either thing.

"Um… Mom, Dad… this is Damian… he's… well…"

"I'm her soul mate," Damian finishes for me, seeing as I keep stammering. I watch as the blood drains from their faces. Neither of them moves a muscle. "Mr. and Mrs. Rae, would you both mind if we go inside and sit down? There is something I must tell you about what happened during the witch hunts." That snaps my mom out of her disbelieving trance.

"What do you mean?" she asks walking toward us, dragging my father behind her.

"There is more to the story than just what you told Serena. And it has a very large impact on Serena and I," Damian says as he turns to walk back to the house when my mom reaches the gate. I smile at my mom from over my shoulder. I still have a hold on Damian's hand and my mom does not miss that. She is starting to look like she might be okay with this. For that I am glad, because I am really starting to believe that I will be more than okay with this. Especially when the emotional rollercoaster stops.

I'm not going to lie though, the whole 'it has a large impact on Serena and I' part is really scaring me. The past two days have been scary. Learning that *I* am a witch. That what I learned about the witch hunts in school is only part of the story, and that my soul mate happens to be a vampire. It is all enough to give a girl an ulcer.

A comfy couch and a cup of hot chocolate sounds really good about now. We walk into the back door that leads into the kitchen followed closely by my parents. I leave Damian standing next to the counter so I can make some hot cocoa. He walks over to the fridge to look at the picture of my parents and me this past summer in Williamsburg, Virginia.

"Do you want anything, Damian?" I ask, not wanting to be rude, then I stop, realizing what I had asked. I really need to pay more attention. I look over at him to see him watching me with a smile.

"Yes, Seri, I can have hot chocolate, which sounds great. And yes, I can answer all the other questions that are unmistakably running through your beautiful mind," he laughs as he comes up to me and kisses my forehead. My knees go weak and I would have crumbled to the floor if he wasn't there to hold me up and make sure I didn't make a mess.

I finish making the hot cocoa while Damian collects some cookies. We turn back to my parents with a tray ready to go to find them staring at us with their jaws on the floor. "What?" I ask. My mom recovers first, getting a smile on her face that brightens her eyes.

"You really are soul mates! Do you realize what just happened?" she asks. I look at Damian who looks at me, thankfully he looks just as confused as I am.

"No," we answer together. I look over to my dad trying to see in his eyes the answer. My dad looks as though he is contemplating where to hide a body. Well, that is just great.

"You two are in sync with each other. You never got in the other's way. You talked before you knew what the other was going to need. You two were like a choreographed dance." She walks away smiling, dragging dad behind and leaving us to follow. Damian and I stare at each.

"Oh my... she... is right," I say, and Damian just smiles that lopsided smile that I am coming to love.

We walk to the living room and Damian sets the tray on the coffee table as we all get settled.

Damian sits on the couch beside me while my mom perches herself on the arm of the chair my dad sits in. "I guess first I should tell you that it wasn't the Birch family that went after the witches. When the family figured out what Melinda was doing, they banished her. You see, Melinda had fallen in love with a vampire named William Crate. Now, William was a nasty thing that cared for nothing and no one. He wanted power because he thought that would get him on the Grand Council and one day the seat of the Grand Master."

"Wait, what is the Grand Council?" I ask.

"The Grand Council is a group of seven vampires including the Grand Master that governs all vampires. It is not easy to join the Grand Council, you must challenge a member and kill them. To outright challenge a Grand Master is suicide. The current Grand Master has held the seat for 600 years. William knew this and thought that a powerful witch standing by his side would guarantee a win. He wanted your ancestor, Elizabeth, but as you said, she had her soul mate, she was married. Besides, I had the honor of meeting her once, she was a smart woman and would not have been easily swayed. But that was okay, because he then met Melinda. She was lonely and easily manipulated. He told her that their love was frowned upon, which it was not, but that if she was to gain enough power and help him become Grand Master, they could be together. So that is what they did. Everything was falling into place for William.

"What William did not know was that the Council had been suspecting that a vampire was helping Melinda. He didn't know that they had eyes on him. Me actually." That had my jaw dropping. I have a million questions, but he gives me a look that said later, so I hold my tongue.

"Their plan was working. Witches were beginning to fear Melinda and vampires were starting to see the power William had over the powerful witch. Before it could go too far though, I was told to bring them in. I was young when all this was happening, William had a good 200 years on me. I let him know I was coming for him, that the Council wanted to see him. By the time I got to him, he had already killed Melinda. He didn't run because he thought he could out-power me. William was arrogant," he says simply. "He never considered who had turned and trained me. He tried to goad me, saying that they sent the lap dog when they should have sent the guard dog. So, I brought him to the Grand Master, with minor injuries. He was sentenced to death for his crimes against the Council and for the death of Melinda. The witches though were told that another witch family had been able to overpower the Birch family. We let them think the story spreading around was true. The

Council decided that the truth of a vampire's part in what happened was better left in the dark because they didn't want a repeat of it."

"What does this have to do with us?" I ask, already suspecting the answer but not wanting to believe it. Damian turns to me on the couch, grabbing my other hand and bringing them both to his lips. The sensation that travels through my body calms me oddly enough, but there is sadness and regret in his beautiful eyes.

"The council was trying to figure out how to handle the aftermath of William and Melinda's love affair. They called me in and asked my opinion because I was out on the streets. I had seen firsthand what had happened to all because of them." He paused looking at me with so much pain. "I told them I thought that it wasn't safe to have two such powerful beings together in any way other than profession. They agreed, and a law was passed for all vampires. No relationships with any supernatural beings." Right there, that is what I was afraid of. And if that wasn't enough, "The punishment is death," he adds.

And with that, my newly-formed world shatters. For the third time today I can't breathe, my throat closes harder than it had before. Damian can't die, the thought alone sends a pain straight to my heart. I barely know him but the thought of him not being here is simply not an option. Over my dead body will I allow anyone to harm him!

Chapter 7

"Serena! Breathe!" he has his hands on the side of my face and forces me to look into his eyes. What I see in those eyes is enough to throw me back into a panic. He is scared; Damian, a powerful vampire, is scared. "Yes, I'm scared, but it will be okay, we have each other." He is right, we do. He leans his forehead against mine and closes his eyes; I follow his lead. "Breathe," he whispers, so I do. I take in a lung full of Damian. Sweet, woodsy, Damian.

When I regain my ability to breathe, I take in a deep breath and I say as I put my hands on either side of his face to force him to look at me, "You can't die, Damian."

"She is right. Your lives are forever intertwined. You die, she dies. And vice versa. Simply because your bodies, your souls, would shut down from loss. You are whole now, you can't go back," my mom says in a matter-of-fact voice. Laced in pain.

We all sit, not moving and not speaking. On the bright side, we don't have to worry about the Birch family. But now we have to worry about the Council, so I guess there really isn't a bright side. I can see that Damian is thinking of something so I lean back and ask, "What are you thinking?"

Damian grabs my hands, squeezing. "We could go to the Council." I can't help but let out a slightly panicked laugh.

"Yes, let's head straight into the lion's den, that way, they won't have to waste the energy to come after us. It will really just save time. Wait…" That is when what he had said earlier clicked. William didn't think about who had turned and trained him? The Council sent him to watch, then bring in William? They asked his opinion even though he was not on the Council? I look over at Damian, he had been giving me a look that said, 'sarcasm isn't helping.'

"Who turned you?" That question has him looking nervous and a little shocked that I thought to ask. Not good.

"Cornelius Gray, Grand Master. He has been training me to take over."

"Wait, he has been training you to kill him?" I ask in a high-pitched, panicked voice that is becoming common with me as of late. I am not liking that.

"Cornelius is old, very, very old. He is not ready yet, but he wants to know that whoever will take over is good for the Council and vampires as a whole. That doesn't mean that he will be easy on me in the fight. He wants to know I am ready and if I can't beat him, then I'm not ready. That also doesn't mean that he will take this well." Great, I got a little excited but I guess not. Really, Grand Master?!

"What will he do to us? And if you lose the fight, that means you're dead! I thought I already made it clear that I don't like that!"

"It isn't going to happen any time soon, Seri, I promise. Besides, even if he decided that tomorrow is the day, I am ready," he says, trying to show me the truth of his words through his eyes. He does believe that he is ready, I just hope that I am when the time comes. "And I think that if we were to tell him that we are soul mates and had no choice in it, then he would test us. Instead of killing us outright." A test, really!? Damian laughs and I look at him stunned. This is not a time for laughing. What is with the people in my life smiling and laughing when I want to scream and cry? "Sorry, your face was priceless. You looked so annoyed."

I pull my hands out of his and cross them over my chest, "Yes, okay, the word test annoys me." I swat his arm just for good measure and in retaliation he starts tickling me.

"That is the second time you have hit me!" he growls.

"Uncle, uncle, you win." I laugh out.

"Good," he answers, relaxing back into the couch. I needed that. I sit up and look at him on the couch to see that he knew I did.

"Thank you." I bring his hand to my lips and kiss his palm. Feeling his skin on my lips sets them on fire.

"Anytime," he answers breathless. Huh…interesting.

I don't know how long we sat there staring at each other but my dad had apparently had enough. He clears his throat, making us both jump, looking over to him. To be honest, I had completely forgotten they were even there. Once again, I really need to focus and pay attention.

My dad looks annoyed and my mom looks near to bursting with that smile. I guess she has come around rather quickly to the idea of me spending my life with Damian, no matter how short that might be. Well, that is a depressing thought, Serena, nice.

"So what kind of test?" my dad asks. He is clearly not happy at all about the whole situation. I doubt he would be no matter who was sitting next to me, though. Poor Dad, he was barley okay with the idea that my soul mate was coming, wanting me to stay his little girl forever. But not only did he come a lot faster than any of us thought, but he is a vampire too. My dad wants nothing more than to grab me and run away, I can see it in his eyes, but he knows firsthand how hard that would be.

"Well…" Damian is quiet for a moment, contemplating the many ways one can be tested by a vampire Grand Master. I had just started to think that he didn't know or that there is just too many to choose one; really, when had I become a masochist? "The only test I can think of that he would be ready to give and that would test both me *and* Serena, is the lock-up test."

"What is that?" I ask, a little nervous and not actually wanting to know. I mentally slap myself. Enough whimpering, Serena; you are a witch, dammit! Not that I know what all that means yet.

"He will lock us in a room together and then starve me."

"That sounds pleasant." Okay, that came out a little sarcastic, fine, really sarcastic, and a bit cynical. Damian gives me that puckered-up crooked smile that clearly says I'm not helping. "I fail to see how that would test me, or you for that matter. That just sounds painful to you," I say, not understanding. Starving Damian would just hurt him, right? I still did not know enough about vampires to know that.

"That would work, honey," my mom answers before Damian can. I turn to look at her. "By starving Damian, that would bring his most basic instinct to the forefront. He would attack any blood source to survive. The same goes for you as well. By putting you in a room where a vampire is that far gone, your powers will be in control, ready to protect."

"Wait. How is that possible? I am not like a vampire, my powers are controlled by reason, not instinct, right?" That is what I assumed, that is how it is described in all the books and movies. Though I guess those aren't the most reliable sources of information.

"Yes and no. In most cases that is true, but when your fight or flight instinct kicks in, your subconscious takes over and your powers will do what is needed to protect you." She raises her hand to stop my question, which is getting annoying. "Against a human it is different. We witches look at humans as…children, in a way. They are ignorant and need our understanding and protection. In most cases, against a human we can protect ourselves without using any powers or just a minimal amount. But a vampire…not so much. Being soul mates though, it would be impossible for you to harm each other, no matter how hungry he is or afraid you are. Theoretically." She just had to add that, didn't she?

"Theoretically? Really, Mom, you had to add that?" I turn to look at Damian. "We really can't run?" I ask, not at all hopeful. Damian gets the saddest look in his eyes.

"We wouldn't last long or get far. I'm sorry. I really think going to Cornelius is our best chance."

"And hope for the best," I finish for him.

"Yes, and hope for the best."

Well, it sounds like we have no other choice. Wonderful!

It's three in the afternoon when we get done talking. We decide to wait until tomorrow to go to Cornelius. This way Damian and I can talk and get to know each other without the stress of being locked in a cage together. Okay, I am sure it is not a cage. Being in the garden has better vibes, that's all. Mom and Dad go back to work in the greenhouses while Damian and I go to the bench under the weeping cherry tree. There is still so much we don't know about each other, which makes sense, we have only known each other for a few hours. No matter how it feels.

It's weird, everyone has heard *someone* say that it feels like they have known a person all their life but really it has only been a short time. Never did I think that they were serious, I mean really, how can that be? But I get it now. It is more a feeling of understanding the other person on such a deeper level that time is inconsequential. I can look into Damian's eyes and know what he is feeling. I can feel what he is feeling. I can listen to him speak and feel his words seep to my bones and I am there with him. Truly an amazing way to feel about someone, to feel *with* someone.

"So, fang boy… movies, right or no?" I ask trying to sound as casual as possible, but really, I never thought that would be something I would ever have to ask. Damian laughs and I smile; secretly I was hoping for that. I love his laugh.

"Somewhat. We don't age. We drink blood but we can eat normal food too. Religious objects don't affect us. We live fairly normal lives. Just like humans, there are the good ones and the bad ones. We are pretty good at policing our own." By this point I am sitting length wise on the bench, my back against his front with his arms around my shoulders. He is holding my hand, running his fingers ever so slightly over my palm, tracing the lines. Also, by this point I can no longer feel my arm, the tingles have completely taken over. I am fighting the shivers that want to slide down my back, and he is chuckling. Dammit, he knows how he is affecting me.

With my brain not functioning correctly, I ask, "Do you have to kill when you feed?" Thank the Goddess because he laughs.

"No, a bite doesn't turn you and we can't drain a person, way too much blood. Besides, we drink bagged blood, we have since it became possible to. We only bite in emergencies. And before you ask, no we are not cursed, soulless creatures. Think of a vampire as someone with an infection that just happens to make us faster, stronger, and live forever or as close as a person can get." After a few minutes of me just sitting there lost in my own head, Damian gets restless or maybe nervous. "Serena? What's wrong?" he asks, placing his mouth next to my ear and whispering. I cannot control the shiver that runs down my back if my life depended on it that time.

I sit up and turn to him. "I'm scared, Damian, I just found out yesterday that I'm a witch. And how do I know for sure that I am, what if it skipped me? I don't know how to fight, I don't know how to be your equal. I can't protect you. I..." Damian grabs my face and shushes me, he actually shushes me. "No, Damian, I don't know who I am anymore and that scares me. I have always been confident and sure and now..."

"You are Serena Rae, that has not changed. You just have a new part of you that you need to learn about, that's all. And I will be right here helping you. You are the same person, Serena. Even if you weren't a witch, and you are, it did not skip you, you know that, you *are* my equal."

"But what if something happens to you because I am not strong enough?"

"It won't, Serena, I will be fine. I am more worried that something will happen to you. I promise, though, nothing will happen to you, I won't let it." He pulls me to him and I lay my head on his chest. I block everything else out but the rise and fall of his chest and the fast, steady beat of his heart. He is right, I need to believe in myself and in him. Together we will be fine. When the hell did I become this needy person? I am not needy; okay, maybe not needy as much as scared. I really don't like this feeling of not knowing in the slightest what will come of all this. There has just been so many changes since yesterday and even this morning.

I take a breath and close my eyes. When I open them, a sense of calm washes over me. He is right, I am a witch. What I woke up to this morning is proof enough. I am strong enough, I always have been, and with Damian, my strong vampire, by my side, I can do anything. Damn but things have just turned upside down.

Chapter 8

We sat like that for a while. I could stay here for all eternity. It is nice to just feel comfortable with someone.

We are so wrapped up in each other that we didn't even hear them coming. We really need to work on that. "How about pizza?" my dad asks and we both jump at the sound of his voice and then my stomach caught up and growled. I haven't eaten since this morning. Damn, I didn't even realize that.

Damian laughs. "Sounds great, Mr. Rae."

That reminds me. "Dad, why did you take Mom's name? I have always wondered but never thought to ask." I know; weird, why would I ask after eighteen years? Honestly though, I didn't even know that he had until about a year ago. Sam and I were going through some of my parents' old yearbooks and saw that my dad was Gregory Shepherd. I always meant to ask but... life, you know. It isn't my dad who answers, he turns to my mom, giving her a 'you want to take this one' look, then walks to the house to order the pizza.

"It is rare nowadays for a witch to marry a witch, in that case you hyphen the names. But when a witch marries a human, the human takes the witch's name."

"Why?"

"Because a name holds a lot of power, Seri. When a witch, or any supernatural beings, hears the name Rae, they know who we are and what we are capable of."

Wouldn't that work for vampires, too? I look over at Damian. I see in his eyes that he knows where my thoughts are going. Before I can say anything, my stomach growls again.

"Later." He laughs.

I had thought that we were going to go inside and wait for the pizza but my mom stops on the patio and turns to Damian. "Damian, why don't you go sit in the chairs over there. Seri, we are going to train while we wait for the pizza." OH, not sure what I am feeling right now.

"Serena?" I hear from the patio doors. Oh shit, Sam. I should have known the voice but I was way too distracted to have even realized it.

"Crap! I completely forgot to call you! I am so sorry, Sam!" she isn't listening though. Her eyes have found Damian and her jaw is now on the patio.

"What is Damian Drake still doing here?" she asks looking over at me, absolute shock and jealousy in her once beautiful blue eyes. Ruined for me forever, damn him.

"Drake? DRAKE?!" My mom and I say as one, though her voice overpowered mine with the shock.

"Yes. Drake," he says, giving my mom a look of warning. I see on my mom's face that she knows the name. Not surprising since he works for the Council. But the look that is on her face says so much more.

"We had other things to worry about than my last name." He laughs, coming to stand beside me. Still, that is a pretty basic and important question to just forget about. Here I am thinking about what we are going to do with our last names when we marry and I don't even know his. And who is to say that we will even get married, just because this feels right doesn't mean it is. Aw crap, my life has become a Carrie Underwood song.

"What happened today? All I got was a cryptic message saying that you had to go home. And that Damian was giving you a ride," Sam asks, trying and failing to pry her eyes away from Damian. I get that.

"Oh… Well…"

"We thought that one of the braces was bad in one the greenhouses and asked Serena to come home to help. She was with Damian when we called and he offered to give her a ride home and stayed to help out," my mom lied, flawlessly, which is creepy. I guess being a witch you would need that talent. Note to self: work on that.

I turn away from my mother and look at Sam who has managed to look away from Damian. "Sorry, Sam, I can't go out tonight."

"That's okay, we got slammed with homework which is going to take me all night to do. I brought you yours by the way. Sorry, Damian, I didn't know you were still going to be here or I would have brought yours too." Sam gives me a pointed look while she says that and I get the message loud and clear. I am so going to hear about this later, and she is expecting a full report from me as well.

"That is alright, Sam, I didn't realize I would still be here either," Damian says with a smile which gets Sam's full attention; I elbow him in the ribs. He leans into his stomach and acts like it hurt, which I know it hadn't. He walks back over to his chair and sits down laughing.

"What is going on here? I feel like I am missing something." If only I could tell her. I feel horrible, she is my best friend.

"Sorry, Sam, I will have to talk to you later. We are a little busy." Sam looks at me trying to hide the hurt in her eyes. I let her see how sorry I am. I go over and give her a hug. "Later," I whisper.

"Promise?"

"Absolutely." Sam says goodbye and walks back through the house; when the front door closes, a tear runs down my face. Damian is there to wipe it away before it even reaches my jaw and I am engulfed in his arms when I break down. Damn, I am never like this. Everything is changing so fast, I can't keep up. I just lied to my best friend, I can't tell her anything. I hate that. In that moment, everything hits me. All the changes that have ripped through my life the last two days drag me down. I have tried to focus so wholly on the one good thing, Damian, but by doing so I lost sight of the worst part. I can't tell Sam. What I feel will become my entire life, will have to be kept a secret from her. My best friend, my sister.

"Shh, I know, Seri, I'm sorry." I just want to crash. Before I know what is happening, my knees buckle and instead of trying to catch me, Damian goes down with me making sure that we land on the patio softly and just held me there. My head on his chest and arms wrapped around him, I hold on tight. He doesn't say anything after that, just rubs my back and hair and places kisses on my head, rocking me. It is comforting, no tingles, no shivers, just peace. A whole new side to the soul mates' business.

My mom must have gone inside because I watch as she comes out of the house with two plates of pizza. She sets them down on the patio next to us and then walks back in without a word. Once again, my stomach growls, and Damian laughs. "Hey, I haven't eaten since this morning, give me a break."

"There you are," Damian says, leaning back to look at me with a smile. He wipes at my cheeks with the back of his knuckles. "You okay?"

"Yes, I'm sorry, I'm usually not like this," I say, picking up the plate so I don't have to look at him. I am so embarrassed.

Damian lifts my chin with his knuckle so I have no choice but to look him in the eye. "I have been waiting for it," he says with sadness and understanding in his eyes. He laughs when I look at him surprised and disgusted. "Serena, with everything that has been thrown at you in the last 24 hours, you have the right to break down. It's healthy to." I guess he is right, but still.

Instead of saying something, I take a bite out of my pizza; damn I am hungry. I just want to shove the whole thing in my mouth but I fight back the urge. Damian must have seen the struggle on my face because he laughs. "Like I said, I haven't eaten since this morning." That just makes him laugh harder. We could have gone inside to eat but I really do not have the strength to move; he must have seen that too because when I am done with the two slices and celery sticks on my plate, he takes it from me and goes inside. He comes back out a minute later with the plate full again. Bless him.

Now that I am not so hungry and there is not a chance I will eat my hand, Damian starts to ask me questions. The getting-to-know-you kind of stuff.

Favorite color: blue; corny, I know, but good gravy sakes, his eyes would make anyone change their color opinions. Him: green, not thinking or wishing too much on that.

Favorite food: Italian. Him: Italian. "You sure it's not blood?" I ask, causing me to once again get the 'really?' look. I just can't help it.

Favorite music: country. Him: jazz. Did not see that coming but I like jazz too, so okay.

Favorite show: *Psych*. Him: *Psych*. We have a laugh at that and talk about our favorite episodes. He tells me how he loves detective shows and books. Perfect, so do I.

It is nice to learn these little things. And as it turns out, we have a lot in common. Maybe the universe does know a thing or two about match-making.

Chapter 9

It starts to get dark out and before I know it, the lights in the garden turn on. They are wrapped all throughout the trees and bushes. Looking like the night sky in front of you. The lights twinkle softly on a dimming timer.

Damian stands up and just stares at the twinkly stars. Standing beside him, he grabs my hand and begins to walk to the garden gate. He pushes it open and we walk through the sparkling lights, ending at our bench. Our bench, I like that. The weeping cherry tree is the center of the garden and has lights all through it. I always thought that it was the best part of the garden at night. We don't sit at the bench but stand under the tree looking at the lights. "Amazing," he whispers.

"Yeah, my mom helped a lot with the lights. I couldn't get them all up without her help."

"So, you told her where to put them?"

"I had this vision of the whole garden. I wanted to make it feel like a fairy world." I nod, looking up at the lights twinkling on the branches throughout the weeping cherry.

"Serena, I understand you don't want to take full credit for this garden because you had help here and there, but you need to. You are as amazing and beautiful as this garden.

You created this place of pure beauty and magic." He has his warm, soft and sure hands cupping my face again, making me consider his eyes. The truth shines through his beautiful blue glowing eyes. That is the last logical thought I have because his eyes have gone from adoration to want. They drift down to my lips and I am lost. He is so sweet, and so gorgeous, perfect. His thumbs are gently gliding up and down my jaw, his fingers in my hair.

Damian steps closer and my hands grab hold of his shirt at his sides to steady myself. I can't breathe. My world starts tipping and tilting.

His lips are so close to mine, I can feel his heated breath wisp across my face. Then he is gone. My eyes had closed and they pop open when his hands leave me.

He hadn't stepped so far out from me that my hands left his shirt but I still felt cold without his heat. "What?" I ask, trying not to sound hurt or breathless and failing miserably at both.

He runs his knuckles gently down my cheek. "I'm sorry but your mom is calling." Well, that's a killjoy. Figures. "She wants us back so you can practice." That also figures. Dammit, I was so close to getting that amazing kiss that I have wanted all day. I am really starting to get frustrated. I turn to head back but Damian grabs my arm and spins me around to face him. He wraps his other arm around my back, effectively pulling me so close I am completely molded to his entire body, and I feel at home. A sense of complete and total peace sweeps through me and my heart rate slows to a steady beat. I can breathe for what feels like the first time in my life. I open my eyes and see it all reflected in his.

His hand lets go of my arm and dives into my hair and around to the back of my neck, pulling me up. His lips are so close to mine, but they never meet. My mom calls and I hear her this time. We pull away and look at each other. Damian laughs and so do I.

"Do you think if we ignore her, she'll go away?"

"Damian! Serena!! If you two do not come here right now, I will start a tornado in there!!"

"No, I don't," Damian says, letting me go and grabbing my hand instead, dragging me to the house. Dammit. Damian turns before we reach the gate, looks at my still flushed face, and shakes his head. "Damn," he says with such feeling, I laugh. "Not funny," he growls. Yeah, it is.

My mom is standing at the gate tapping her toe. "Sorry, Mom, we got caught up talking about the lights," I lie, but she knows that.

"Of course you did," she says with utter disbelief turning away, "you two have lasted a lot longer than your father and I did, I have to give you that."

"Mom, I so don't want to know that!" I meet her in the middle of the patio, leaving Damian on the edge in a chair. She sits down so I follow suit.

"Close your eyes and breath. Look within yourself and find the fire, the passion, the heart of you. That is where your powers rest."

"You sound like Yoda, Mom," I laugh.

"Serena Elizabeth Rae! Concentrate! This is not a joke." When she looks at me and sees that I really am not going to take that seriously, she says, "Alright, it may be easier if you close your eyes and think of Damian, find him within you. He doesn't just amplify your power. A witch's power is tied to their emotions. What you feel for your soul mate will always be your strongest emotion. Find him and you find your power." That I can do... I think. I can't just go searching inside myself without looking for something tangible.

So, with one last look at Damian to see his encouraging smile and silly wink, the butterflies begin to flutter and I close my eyes and search inside myself. Diving deep into my emotions: fear that tomorrow won't go well, confusion over everything I have learned, newly felt pride over being part of the Rae legacy, and finally love. What I find astounds me. When Mom said look for the fire, the passion, the heart within, she wasn't kidding. What I find within me is a big orb that looks like a flaming ball of fire. The emotions coming off from it are clear; I am falling in love with Damian and I have only known him a few hours. But then again, I was in love with him the moment I saw him; love at first sight really can happen I guess. Now that I am getting to know him though, I can't help it.

The orb abruptly turns into the color of Damian's eyes. A bright blue that swirls and glows even brighter. I feel like it will consume me. But I am not afraid.

I could just say that I found it and let my mom tell me what to do, but I know what to do. I don't know how, I just do.

I imagine my hands grabbing the orb knowing that this love, that Damian will never burn me. I take the orb and expand it. I want to show my mom, show Damian, that I found my power and that I am not afraid of it. I push it out to surround me in its blue fiery light. When I open my eyes, it is to see my mom standing in front of me with Damian at her side, both looking stunned.

"Found it," I say, looking at them through the fire. Then I realize that I am looking them in the eyes. I look down to see the ground five feet below me. Holy crap! I let my feet instinctively drop. They don't touch the ground but remain a few inches above it and the orb expands to surround my feet and legs. "Whoa!"

"Serena, that is amazing. I have never seen a power orb that bright before and how did you know I wanted you to do that?" my mother asks walking around me.

"What do you mean? Is it really that bright?" I ask. It looks bright but I didn't think that it would be brighter than normal. Now that I think about it, I wouldn't know. "You wanted me to find my power, I did. I thought I would show you instead of telling you. And look, it is the same color as Damian's eyes."

I turn to Damian. He walks to me and smiles as he considers my eyes. Before I know it, the smile fades. "Serena, your eyes!" Without thinking, Damian reaches his hand out, instantly I am scared that the fire will burn him, I can feel the heat coming off from it.

Instead of burning him, the orb uses his outstretched hand and pulls him in, surrounding him with me. Now we are standing off the ground together, the orb around us. As soon as my power has us both, the color of the fire changes. No longer is the fire a bright blue swirl but blue and green, molding and conforming together into a beautiful pattern fitting perfectly. "It looks like your eyes!" That surprises me enough to look at Damian. I gasp throwing my hand over my mouth. "What, Serena?" I can't answer him for a minute, too shocked.

"Damian, it looks like your eyes!" What the hell is going on? Damian looks surprised by that but when he sees that I am beginning to get afraid, he pulls my hand away from my mouth and replaces it with his lips. The kiss is scorching. I don't see the orb getting stronger or brighter around us as it blocks out the world, but I feel it. His lips are the fire feeding my soul.

He licks and nips my lower lip, asking for me to open to him, I do. He tastes like strawberries and cream. How is it that even possible? My arms are around him, pulling him closer. Deeper. His hands are on my hips keeping me firmly planted against him. Damn, this is…no words. Then I feel it, the orb closing in, seeping into my bones. The fire runs through me like a hot river of energy. Not hurting as much as shocking me. He pulls back with one last kiss, placing his forehead against mine, his eyes closed. "Did you feel that?" I ask.

The orb starts to slowly fade, dropping us to the ground. "Yes, what was that? It felt like the fire was diving into my veins. I actually felt your power run through me, it felt like electricity. But it didn't hurt," he adds in a confused tone.

"For me it felt like pure energy, but it was weird though, it didn't feel like mine." My parents are by the door watching. When our feet hit the ground, no one moves. No one speaks. Damian and I don't break apart, we stand and stare at each other. I am amazed by his eyes. They were beautiful before but now they are spectacular. Never have I seen more amazingly beautiful and bright eyes. And apparently mine are now the same.

After a few minutes, my mom walks to us. "Serena? Damian? Are you two okay?" We don't even bother looking at her. We both nod yes, never taking our eyes off each other. "That was miraculous! Now that you found your power, do you have the energy to test it?" she asks. After that kiss, I could run a marathon.

"Mom, do you know what just happened? Why have our eyes changed color?" I ask, looking to her so she can see for the first time, I am assuming since she hasn't shown any sign of seeing them.

Just as I thought, her eyes go wide and she stammers. There is the response I have been waiting for. "Oh my…um no, honey. That is not normal." I gathered that. "It must have something to do with both of you being supernatural. Let's focus on that later."

"Um…why…? This really seems like something that we should figure out now, don't you think?"

"There is no way of learning any more about that other than living it. I will ask around to see if anyone else has ever had or heard of this happing." I guess she is right, but I don't like having one more thing we have to wait for.

I walk around Damian to the edge of the patio by the garden gate. I turn towards them and imagine all the furniture in my hands. I begin to lift them off the ground. Then I imagine myself rising. I float into the air. To be honest, this feels right. This feels like I have been doing it all my life. I just *know* what to do and how to do it. "Wonderful, Serena, just…wonderful. It looks like you have it covered for now. You know what you are doing well enough to get through the next few days."

"Oh, you think I am ready to go in front of the Grand Master of the Vampire Council?"

"You are a natural, Serena. More than that, you are not going to be alone. That is… I am so proud of you!" She looks ready to cry. My dad comes up behind and wraps her in his arms, watching me. He looks ready to cry too. They look so proud. Today is a crying day it seems, great.

I am able to gently put the furniture back on the patio before I lose my focus and start falling. I don't need to worry; Damian is there, before I even come close to the ground, to catch me. I knew he would, but damn he moves fast.

I laugh, I can't help it. Hey, it's better than crying, "What's so funny, you could have gotten hurt!" Damian chides.

"No, I couldn't have! I knew you would catch me."

"You're right, I will always catch you, but still, don't do that again."

"Alright, I promise," I say and he kisses me, just a small one but still, heaven.

"When you get back, we will work on spell-casting. That is a little harder," my mom says before turning with my dad and walking inside. Damian and I follow.

My parents go to the office while we go to the couch. We settle in and start talking. We are still getting to know each other. Seriously, Damian has over four hundred years' worth of stuff to fill me in on! I look up to the clock a little later and nearly jump off the couch. "It's 9 already? How long were we in that orb making out?" I ask looking at Damian.

He laughs so hard he rolls off the couch. I can't help but laugh with him. "What is so funny?"

"Serena, you don't even realize what just happened do you?" he laughs. I am so confused. "My little witch," he says getting up on his knees and placing himself between my legs, "you didn't say anything, you projected that thought to me. Actually, you threw that to me."

"Seriously?"

"Soul mates can do that, honey. Not all witches can read minds like I can. But all soul mates of witches can talk mind to mind. It helps keep us connected," my mom answers coming into the living room. How does she do that? I look up to ask but she is already gone. Really?

"How do we even do that?" I ask looking to him.

"There is what feels like a chain that connects you. You follow that," my mother once again says, popping into the living room, this time from the kitchen. How? How does she do that sneaking thing?

"Serena?" I look to Damian with that call, *"Are you okay that we can do this?"* he asks without opening his mouth. With his voice flowing through my mind, I feel the chain.

Mind to mind, how do I feel about him being in my head? We can't change it, and seeing that it feels warm and peaceful having him speak to me like that.

"How does it feel to have me in your mind even if it is just to talk?" I ask instead.

"Complete, like you have been missing all my life. That seems to be how it feels with everything to do with you."

I like that. He is right, that is the peaceful feeling.

"Good, and yes I am okay with it," I say in answer to his previous question, putting my hands in his silky, shaggy brown hair. How does he get his hair to look like it's purposely messy and oh-so-very sexy. Damian laughs. *"Okay, so this is going to take getting used to,"* I thought to him. I bring his lips to mine to stop the laughing.

Chapter 10

"Serena, enough," Damian says in my mind, breathless. I don't listen but deepen the kiss instead. *"You're killing me!"* he whines and I laugh against his lips. "I have to call Cornelius," he says still against my lips. Ugh, fine.

"Way to ruin the moment," I say, turning my head away from him with a secret smile. He answers by nipping at my ear. I can't fight the shiver that runs through my entire body.

Damian drops his head to my knee. "Don't do that, do you have any idea how sexy that is?" I burst out laughing. "You are evil, my little witch." That just makes me laugh harder. "Alright," he says getting up and sitting next to me, "time to get serious." I give him a pouty look. Damian stares at me. "Evil, pure evil," shaking his head he moves over to the chair.

"Hey!"

"Oh no, I am staying over here until I get this call over with, I don't need you making my mind wonder."

"But it's fun!" Damian burst out laughing. I love making him laugh, it is becoming a fun pastime that makes my bones melt. "Alright, I will be good."

"I doubt that," he says with a crooked smile and a raised eyebrow.

With an extra sweet smile, I say, "You're right, but I will try my hardest."

He sits there staring at me until finally he asks, with suspicion written across his sexy face, "What are you planning?"

"Are you going to make that call?" I ask sweetly.

Damian just watches me until he decides that I'm not going to cave. He starts to dial as he looks away but before he presses send, he looks at me. "You don't need to say anything; he will know there is a human with me, and Serena," he says looking straight through me, "no talking dirty in my head." He smiles.

"Oh, well played, Mr. Drake, well played," I say as serious as I can. When he winks at me though, I lose it. "Before you call though, what do you do in Ithaca?" I had been wondering and I'd rather know before the call, no surprises.

"Cornelius owns a security company, I work for him, Gray Security." Oh well, that seems like a good job for vampires.

"A sexy macho job," I send to him.

"Things like that, Serena, that is very distracting," Damian growls.

"I couldn't help it, you walked right into that one."

He laughs, *"Yes, I did."* Out loud he asks, "You ready?"

I take a deep breath, readying myself for the unknown. I decided something inside that orb with all that power flowing threw me; make the best of what is happening. I can't change my life as it is; I'm a witch and I am the soul mate of a powerful, sexy vampire. I'm looking on the bright side of it all. Damian is sweet, and funny, and sexy as hell.

As for me being a witch, it's an adventure and something I am beginning to think I will love. So, I look to Damian, smile and say, "Hit it."

Damian smiles at me and pushes send. It hadn't even finished the first ring when the other end is picked up. A deep masculine voice that sends a shiver of fear down my back, answers, "Damian! Where have you been?"

"Hello, Cornelius, I'm sorry I have been busy with something. I would actually like to meet with you tomorrow to discuss something important that has come up." There is silence on the other side for a few minutes. I am beginning to get nervous; Damian notices and places a hand over his heart. I know my heart was starting to beat too fast, so I take a deep breath to calm myself, looking straight into Damian's beautiful eyes.

Finally, Cornelius answers, "Okay, Damian. You know I do not like surprises but I hear that this is not something to discuss over the phone. Come see me tomorrow, eleven a.m." Then the line disconnects. We are both silent for a moment.

"Well, that went good," I say in a chipper voice.

Damian laughs. "Yeah, but he is not happy, then again Cornelius is rarely ever happy." He is smiling and it reaches his eyes so I'm not going to worry about it.

He stands up and puts the phone back in his pocket. He walks over to me and holds his hand out to me. Without even thinking about it, I put my hand in his, immediately feeling the heat and peace that his touch always gives me. He pulls me up to him and wraps me in his arms. We stand there holding each other for a while. I listen to his heart beat slow and steady. I soak in the heat that radiates from him.

His hands move up and down my back; I feel like purring right now.

Until Damian pulls back and looks at me. I can see what is coming in his eyes. "I have to go eat, *my* diet. I will be right back, okay?" My heart plummets. My eyes go wide, more out of shock that my body is reacting like this than anything. I knew that he was going to have to leave at some point and as much as that hurt, I didn't have a panic attack thinking of it. "Serena, breathe."

"I know... I'm sorry. I knew you were going to have to leave at some point," I say to him, breathless.

"I know, Serena, that is why I just stood here holding you for a while before saying anything. I was trying to work through the pain it causes to have to leave you. It's okay, I understand, just breathe." He holds my head to his chest, brushing his fingers through my hair, sporadically laying kisses there. Damn, I could fall asleep standing in his arms.

"Okay, go before it gets too hard to let you," I say, pushing out of his arms and feeling like I am pushing my own soul away. He grabs my chin, lifting my face up and places one quick kiss to my lips before he is gone. I don't see him move. I don't see the door open and close, but I feel every step he takes.

I don't know how long I stood there staring at the front door. I feel lost, alone. I just met him but I feel empty without him near. I am not a girl that needs a man by my side, so this is a new feeling for me, and I am not sure I like this part.

"That will fade, honey." I jump at my mother's words. Once again, she is just there.

"How the..."

"Language."

"...heck do you do that?"

"I am not walking any different, Seri. You are different. More like your focus is somewhere else." Sure, blame me.

Well, it is your fault, you should work on that.

"What do you mean by 'that will fade?'" My mom walks over to the couch and sits down, patting the seat next to her.

"When I first met your father, I wasn't ready for the commitment either," she says as I sit.

"Really? That surprises me. You and Dad are so strong, and so... really there are no words." How am I always lost for words lately? I am never lost for words.

"I was like you, Serena. I had plans and dreams. I was so scared that I was not going to get the chance to follow them. I thought that I was going to have to get a house, start a family and, well, grow up. My life was going to be over at 18. When I met him though, everything changed. It is intense, isn't it?"

"That is an understatement." I laugh.

"We had only been together a few hours when he had to leave. Soul mate or not, we were still kids and had to follow the rules. Just like you," she says giving me a pointed look. Message received. "When he drove out of view, I thought I was going to die; my soul cried and my heart ached. It took everything I had not to go after him. I guess it never really fades as much as you learn to handle it. Just know that he feels the same. And you can still talk," she says, pointing to her head.

"I forgot about that!" I say a bit excited. Okay, *really* excited.

86

"And, Serena, you aren't giving up your plans or dreams. The great thing, or one of the great things, about soul mates is that no matter what, they want you to be happy. If going to college, or traveling the world, or whatever you want to do in life, will make you happy, then Damian will want that too. And you for him. In time, you will learn all of this."

"Really, Mom?"

"Yes, Seri." Kissing my cheek, my mom gets up and goes back to the office with my dad. Damian and I haven't really talked about any of that yet or really anything about the future, but I believe her. Kind of like the whole taking over as Grand Maser thing; I don't particularly like it, but if it is what Damian wants, then I will support him.

My legs start to bounce and fidget. "Okay, I can't sit here and wait." I switch to talking in my mind, sending it to Damian. *"Damian, I'm going to take a shower, let yourself in when you get back."* I get up and walk to the bathroom.

When I reach my bedroom to grab clothes, I hear Damian say, *"Do you have any idea how weird it was to hear you say that? I was not expecting that, I damn near jumped and turned to see if you were behind me."* He laughs at me. I can't help but laugh out loud.

"Oh good, I was hoping to scare you," I say trying to hold the laugh back from him.

"I bet you were. Don't worry, I will get you back. You will never see it coming too. Vampires are very sneaky, you know," he says matter-of-factly. I don't think I will ever not have a smile while talking to him.

"You don't scare me, bring it on, fang boy."

"What was it that you said to me earlier, you so did not want to open that can of worms? It's on now, little witch."

Oh, throwing my words back at me! Nice. I laugh at him, *"I'm getting in the shower now, bye!"*

"Oh! You did that on purpose, leaving me with that in my head. Evil little witch, evil!"

"I need to concentrate to take my bra off so I can't talk to you right now. Enjoy your meal, Damian," I send a laugh to him. Mean, I know. I hear him groan in my head, then a growl. I just laugh harder sending that to him.

"You are so going to get it when I get back, Serena Rae! Torture is not nice!"

"I don't see how politely informing you that I am taking a steaming hot shower could be torture. I thought you might like to know. And as for the bra, I was wearing a particularly difficult one that I really did need to focus on, to get off. But I got it off so it's okay now. But I will let you go eat. I'll see you when you get back." I get in the shower and let the spray run down me, hearing Damian's voice run through my head with promises of revenge. I laugh thinking how amazing it is to have him. But I tune him out and focus on the shower. This has always been my me-time. I like to use the water to wash all the stress and worry away.

As I start to wash my hair, my mind wonders once again. My parents are pagan but I never really thought of my beliefs. Meeting Damian has gotten me to think though, or really, to *feel*. I can no longer imagine one God, one part of a whole. Whoever created *us,* created soul mates, must know what it is like. They must know this sense of completion. To think of anyone not having this, is painful. Pagans believe that not only is there Father God but a

Mother Goddess too. To be honest, finding my power has opened my senses. I feel her, the Mother, the Goddess. I can't help but thank her, thank them both for bringing me Damian, for choosing him for me.

I take longer in the shower than usual. Letting all the revelations wash through me. Allowing my mind and body to align, the tension and stress to leave. I breathe and relax.

When I step out, I damn near scream; Damian is back and his voice lets me know as it runs through my head, fully meant to scare me. Damn him, he got me back. I was so focused on relaxing that I lost track of him.

Okay let's play then. *"Oh, good, you're back. How about you pick a movie for us to watch?"* I say in a calm voice not letting him know he scared me.

"Nice try, but I heard your heart speed up and the sharp intake of breath. Can't fool a vampire." Oh, not cool.

"Cheater!" I say; he simply laughs. I am still learning the ins and outs of my new powers, but I open my mind to see him in the living room. I see him laughing and getting ready to sit on the couch. So, I zap his gorgeous butt as he sits down. I laugh as he jumps back up letting him hear it. I close my mind back up to get dressed, feeling as though he can see me even though I know he can't.

"Talk about cheating," he says laughing. Then, in a serious tone, *"Good job."* I hear the pride in his voice which makes my confidence and heart swell.

"Thank you. I will be right out." I dress quickly in my overlarge shirt and gym shorts, not being able to wait any longer to be near him. I grab the brush off the counter before running out the door. I can brush my hair while we watch the movie. I hold myself back as I get out the door and walk

as calmly as I can down the hall. When I get to the living room, Damian is standing by the couch, which makes me stop. He looks up at me and his eyes run slowly down my body. "Okay, enough," I say. Damn tingles. He laughs, "Why are you standing there?" I ask, knowing the answer, so I send a laugh to him.

Chapter 11

"I am so glad you find it funny. I am not sitting down until I know you aren't going to electrocute me again," he says smiling. I burst out laughing so hard, I go to the floor, sending my parents running down the hall.

"What is wrong with her?" one of them asks; I think it was my dad's voice but really, I don't know. I can't hear it very well. I stop long enough to look to Damian, who is watching me with a look that says, 'you are just so proud of yourself aren't you,' and I lose it again.

Damian answers saying, "She zapped me when I went to sit on the couch; from the bathroom, mind you." He sounds so put out that it makes me go into another round of hysterics. "How did you manage that by the way?" he asks, "You couldn't have known I was sitting down."

I really don't know, I just did. I get myself under control enough to stand up, wiping the tears from my eyes. "All I did was close my eyes and open my mind looking for yours. I couldn't hear what you were thinking but I could see what you saw. And it was more of a small zap."

My mom turns to head back with my dad's hand in hers. "She is doing so well!" she says, her voice full of pride. When they are hidden away in the office, Damian crosses the room with vampire speed and pushes me against the wall with the hair brush forgotten on the floor, his lips find mine, and he punishes me greatly.

Note to self: torture and zap his butt at every chance. He lifts me up on the wall and I wrap my legs around his waist. His tongue lashes mine, sending shock waves down my back. When he pulls back, I am good and punished. I can't think, can't talk, and thank god he has me in his arms because my legs are non-existent. He bends to pick up the brush with me still wrapped around him, then he walks us over to the couch and gives me a hard look that helps me find my voice enough to laugh. He smiles as he sits on the couch.

"You do realize that that was not punishment but more like encouragement for more teasing torture and ass zaps, right?" I say as he gets us settled with him sitting horizontal and me in between his legs.

He grabs my hair and gently uses it to pull my head back so I can look at him. He kisses me again, before saying, "I must be a masochist because I really enjoyed that teasing torture, and the zap, well, that just really made me laugh. No, that kiss was simply because I missed you. Plus, that did punish you, your heart hasn't stopped racing. Neither has mine but…" he shrugs. I laugh as I stretch my neck up to kiss him, slowly. His hand is no longer pulling my head back but pushing it up. I could kiss him forever.

He turns his head. "Okay, there is only so much torture I can take." I give him the pouty look. "Evil little witch. Turn around so I can brush your hair before it dries," he laughs. If he hadn't said 'brush your hair,' I wouldn't turn around but I do love to have my hair brushed.

Damian pushes play on the movie and I smile. He has picked one of my favorites, *The Princess Bride.* I know, corny, but I can't help it. It is one of the few romance movies that I like. I think because it has fencing, and danger, and magic, and humor. It's a funny romance. Besides, it seems kind of right to watch right now. Though I have to fight to stay awake long enough to watch it. If Damian brushing my hair isn't distracting enough, he stops half way through the movie and starts to run his fingers in my hair, which really, is worse, at least for my focus. It feels amazing and I have to fight back moans. He knows this of course, I can feel his silent laughter.

As the movie ends, Damian wraps his arms around my neck and holds me close. Putting his lips to my ear, he whispers, "Time for me to go." I have been bracing for it this time. I hold on to his arms around my neck and breathe him in. I never want to forget the feel of his arms and his intoxicating smell enveloping me.

"I know…" I am silent for a minute just soaking him in; his head is resting on my shoulder and I tilt my head into his. When I am strong enough, I stand up, I unwrap myself from him, and walk over to the door. I turn to see him getting up from the couch. He comes over to me and puts his hands into my hair, lifting my face up to his. Stepping close to me he places his forehead on mine. He takes a deep breath in through his nose, then kisses me quickly and is gone. I'm glad that he doesn't linger but makes it quick, and less painful really. The ache and need to follow is strong but manageable.

"I will be back in the morning to get you. Be ready, bring a bag with the essentials in it. Good night, Serena."

"Good night, Damian."

I go to the office to find my parents discussing next year's crops. Most people would be talking about this while sitting in individual chairs. Not my parents; my mom is firmly planted on my dad's lap, leaning on the desk making notes. This is normal; I guess Damian and I will be like this in 20 years, needing to be touching in some way.

But Damian will still look 19. That thought makes me pause. How had I gone all day and not thought about that little, but rather big, problem? Not once? Damian will forever be young and gorgeous while I will age and look like his grandmother. My mom looks over at me and I force a smile walking into the room. "Oh, Serena, did Damian leave, honey? I'm sorry it has to be like this," my mom says, putting down the pen to give me a hug.

"Yes, he left. And I know it does, Mom. It's okay," I say, encasing her in a big hug and not wanting to let go. I am going to the Vampire Council tomorrow, hoping that they will lock me in a room and not kill me instead. So, I have to enjoy this while I can. I breath in my mom's lilac aroma that is all her.

"Oh, Seri. Don't worry, everything will be okay. Damian has been trained to fight Cornelius. With you by his side, well, I am sure the two of you can get out of anything together. You are both so powerful, you will be fine," she says, pulling back to look down at me with a very serious look. She really thinks we can take down the Vampire Council. That makes one of us. I just don't want to find out who is right.

"I know, Mom. But I am new at this. I hope you are right though. I'm going to pack and head to bed. It has been a long day. Or two," I say, trying to sound as if I'm not freaking out completely inside. My hands start to feel warm; looking down at them I half expect to see them at least a little red. That is weird. Mom gives me one more hug. She steps back when my dad stands up. "Goodnight," I say, giving my dad a hug.

"We love you, Seri, and will always be here if you need us."

"I love you too, Daddy. Love you, Mom."

I walk out of the office but instead of going to my bedroom, I go to the back patio. I just need to. When I get outside, I go to the middle of the patio and throw my arms out, letting go. I don't know why, or what is going on, just that I need to loosen the hold that I have on my powers. I hadn't even realized that I had a hold on them.

I guess between thinking about tomorrow and the problems Damian and I are going to have to face with him not aging while I do, put a lot of stress on me. All the stress causes this burning reaction. This needs to release. I am going to need to find a good outlet I guess, but for now... the next thing I know, flames are shooting out of my hands. What is really weird, and yes weirder than the fact that I have flames shooting out of me, is that the flames aren't red but blue and green swirl. It seems that my powers are all about Damian's eyes. I am okay with that, I love Damian's eyes. Although my eyes now match his. This is my life now, people.

The flames recede and I feel ten times better. Note to self: when hands feel like they are burning, you need to go let off some steam. Literally. Oh, that is just too funny.

"Feel better, honey?" my mom asks coming out the patio doors, making me jump.

"Yes, thank you," I answer looking at my hands as if they just appeared.

My mom comes over and kisses my head. "All will be fine, Serena, just watch." With that she turns and goes back inside.

I smile, I must believe and hope that it will be. For now, I need to focus on the present or else I will freak out about the future, and there is no point in worrying about something that hasn't happened yet.

"Damian? You will never guess what just happened" I say getting excited by this. I *really* am beginning to like being a witch. I never know what is going to come next.

"You sound excited so I am guessing something really good?"

"Yes, but that isn't a guess," I inform him laughing.

"Okay, let me see... you found a black cat in your yard and have named him Binks? He doesn't talk, does he?"

"Just for that I am making you watch Hocus Pocus over and over and over and..."

"Okay, okay! I give up, what happened?" he asks.

I look down at my hands and imagine the fire burning in my palm. It works and I smile, sending the image of the fire in my hands and the feeling of pride in making the flame, to Damian. I want him to be a part of what I just accomplished.

Damian doesn't say anything for a minute. When he speaks, it is with awe in his voice, *"Serena, that is amazing! It is rare for a witch to conjure their element with that much control. Definitely not this early"* I think my mom said something like that this morning after finding my sheets singed. *"Serena, I am so proud of you. That is exciting."* Hearing Damian say that sends butterflies soaring in my chest. I can't help the big grin that breaks across my face.

"Thank you. Now I am going to pack and head to bed. I'll see in the morning."

"I can't wait. And Serena…"

"Yes," I say walking back inside and heading to my room.

"No dreams about fires please." I laugh closing my bedroom door. Once again, he walks right into it.

"Of course not, Damian, only dreams about you. Though those could start a fire."

"I really need to watch what I say around you," he says laughing.

"Yes, yes you do. Good night, Damian."

"Good night, Serena."

I am giggling like a little girl as I pack my bag to go with me to meet the Grand Master of the Vampire Council. Damn, I think I am becoming a masochist. Damian does that to me though. He makes me laugh like no one else can. He gets my humor, and he throws it right back at me. He makes me want to think positive and smile about the bad just as much as the good because no matter what happens, I know that he will be right next to me.

I finish packing my bag; tooth brush, comb, underwear, wallet, passport (you never know), socks, PJs, and a change of clothes. I think that should do it. I hope so. What does one take to be locked in a cell with a starving vampire boyfriend? Do they have information packets for this?

Sleep, I need sleep.

I climb into bed and curl up in a ball. I can smell my shirt this way, I can smell Damian on me. I drift off in no time and dream of Damian. His smile and his laugh haunt my dreams, making me feel at peace.

Chapter 12

I wake the next morning feeling like I had slept for days. My body nearly hummed with energy. I stretch and jump out of bed smiling. I dress quickly before running out to the kitchen. I don't stop there though. I run out the door, some part of me being pulled to the garden. I don't stop until I reach the weeping cherry and Damian's waiting arms. Our spot, here under this tree. "Damn. I missed you!" Damian says into my hair. "Do you realize we have only known each other for 24 hours now?" he asks. I pull back and take his wrist. He is right, it is 8 am.

I look up at him stunned. "It feels like years." 24 hours, that is it! That was all it took to fall in love with him.

Wait, what? Did I just think that? I walk away from him and sit on the bench. Do I love him? I look over at Damian. He's watching me, waiting for me to think through whatever is on my mind. The truth is, yes, I do love Damian and that doesn't scare me. I smile. He doesn't think I'm weak when I cry. He makes me laugh and he thinks I'm funny. He isn't scared of what I can do or can potentially do. He is honest and open. That is a rare thing to find. But before I say anything, "Damian, I want to go to college. I want to find my place in the world, and I want to travel. I want to see what is out there." He doesn't say anything but he is clearly surprised by that outburst.

He walks over to me and sits on the bench. He watches me; placing a hand on my cheek, he simply asks, "Where do you want to go to school?"

"Honestly, I don't know. Somewhere new I think. I know that is so vague but that is what I have right know."

"Okay, well, when you figure that out, let me know so I can tell Cornelius where I'm going." That's what I wanted to hear.

I jump into his arms and kiss him. I surprise him again because he falls off the bench with an 'oaf' and starts laughing.

"And if you want to see the world, I can take you anywhere you want to go, just name it." Goddess, thank you, I love this man!

"What about you, Damian? What do you want?" I ask leaning up with my hands on the ground to look him in the eyes.

"Serena, I just want you. You are the last adventure I have been waiting for. I love you," he says looking deep into my eyes, letting ever thing show.

I lean down to give him a scorching kiss. "I love you too," I say against his lips breathless.

We get off the ground and sit at the bench for a while just watching the sun shine through the tree and talking about all the places I want to go. Prague, Cairo, Paris, Budapest, London, Edinburgh, and so many more. Then my stomach growls. "Okay, breakfast time." Damian laughs.

We go inside to find my parents have breakfast already made. Pancakes, sausage, bacon, eggs, hash browns, and best of all, coffee. Yes, I am 18 and drink coffee, sue me. I don't really need coffee this morning but it might help settle my nerves later.

Everything smells amazing. My mom loads up mine and Damian's plates before we are even fully in the door. Setting them down she says, "Okay, eat up, you are both going to need your strength. Damian, is there any way we can know what is going on after the meeting? I would like to talk to you two while you are being tested."

"Well, if that is what Cornelius decides to do, I can ask him to get you a number to reach Serena on, just to check in."

"That would be great, thank you, dear," she says standing on her tippy toes to reach up and kiss Damian on the cheek. What is funny about this is that Damian is far older than my mom.

"Dear," I say to Damian, which makes him smirk.

"That's right, be jealous," he says sitting down. I laugh picking up my fork. My parents sure know how to cook. The best part is that everything is local. Bought right from the farm. I love it, and honestly, it just tastes better. Makes you wonder, is it my parents cooking or just the fresh food? And my mind is wondering again.

"I don't need to be, I'm honey, you're only dear."

"Give me a week and I'll be up to slugger." That makes me nearly choke on my food. It's a good thing that I wasn't drinking my coffee because it would have been coming out of my nose and *that* would have hurt. Both of my parents look over at me with worry while Damian sits trying to control himself. A four-hundred-and-sixty-four-year-old

vampire being called 'slugger,' holy crap I think I could pee myself laughing.

"Serena, are you okay?" my dad asks. He has finally given up trying not to laugh. I kick him under the table to stop him. Of course, that just makes him laugh harder.

"Yes, Dad, I'm fine, thank you," I cough out. Then I send to Damian, *"I will get you back for that."* He simply gives me a wink.

We spend the rest of breakfast talking about the farmstand and what produce we will be selling next year. "Hopefully the newest apple trees will begin to produce next year. A lot of our customers are waiting for those Gala Apples. Oh, and Seri, before you head off to college, we would like your help in hiring someone to take your place. Your mother and I can't work in all the greenhouses and work the stand, and keep up with the flower garden. We are going to need help."

"Okay, as long as you aren't replacing me completely. No renting my room out, or changing it to a workout room that will never be used."

"Ha-ha. Smart…"

"Language," I say in a sing-song voice.

"Damian, are you sure you want to take her?" my dad asks.

"Hey! Absolutely," Damian and I say in unison.

I look at my dad and, having a 5-year-old moment, stick out my tongue at him. I get a smirk back.

"Now who wouldn't want that?" Damian says. So I stick out my tongue at him. *"Are trying to tempt me with a make-out session in front of your parents?"* he jokes.

"You wish."

"For the make-out session? Always. To getting shot by your dad? Not so much. I might not die but it would hurt like hell."

I laugh, which gets my parents to give me a questioning look. This mind-to-mind thing is quite useful.

Damian begins to ask my parents some questions. What colleges they went to? How they ended up in Spencer, N.Y.? And what made them stay? It is nice. I learn some things I never knew. Like my parents happened upon Spencer because they had gotten lost. They fell in love with the area and decided to stay.

Breakfast turns out to be nice and pleasant instead of depressing. I am so glad that my parents are really beginning to warm to Damian, vampire or not.

We sit and talk with empty plates in front of us and the coffee all gone. Until Damian looks at me, "We have to go, Seri." I have been dreading that.

"Okay," is all I can say since I really want to stomp my foot, say no, and go hide in my room. Time to grow up Seri and deal with what has been thrown at you. We all stand up, I walk to my room and grab my bag. Coming back, I find my parents and Damian at the front door. I hand my bag to him and he checks inside. "Good?" I ask.

"Perfect," he says putting his arm around my shoulder and pulling me to him for a quick kiss. Damian says one last good bye and goes out to the car to wait for me.

I look at my parents. They look as they always do, holding each other with smiles on their faces. But those smiles don't reach their eyes as I give them both a big hug and a kiss good bye. Turning away, I can only hope that this will not be the last time I see them.

We drive in silence. Not an awkward silence, just silence. It actually kind of feels like an impending doom silence. Nice, Serena, way to be optimistic. Let's be honest, okay; two days ago, I thought my biggest task this year was getting through all of my free periods without ripping the hair out of my head out of sheer boredom. And then maybe Regents exams. I never prepared or even considered a meeting with the Grand Master of the Vampire Council to ask him not to kill me or my vampire boyfriend. How does one even prepare for that? Make blood pudding as an offering? I can't help but smile at that.

I look over at Damian to see him looking relaxed and with a little smile. "I can feel you worrying." he says squeezing my hand that is in his. He looks at me. "What was that smile for?" That reminder makes me smile again.

We stop at a red light as I say, "I was just wondering if bringing blood pudding as an offering would help." Damian jerks his head over to me with a burst of laughter.

"I think Cornelius is going to like you." That has my eyes going as round as saucers.

"Why do you think that? It would seem to me that he will hate me, if nothing else, I am taking his predecessor."

"You're right, he might think that at first. But then he will see that with you by my side I will be even more ready to take over. And that you have a sense of humor like mine." Okay, I can see that.

"This is all well and good if he lets us live. So whether he likes me or not is moot. But I find that I hope he does like me," I admit. I look out of the window to see that we are in a part of Ithaca that I have never been to. "Where are we going anyway?"

"Up in the hills between Ithaca College and Cornell. We do a lot of security for visiting professors and guest speakers for both schools." That would be why I didn't recognize any thing. I have never been up on the hill. I have no reason to. My parents want me to go to IC or Cornell, like I could ever get into Cornell. I have good grades but not that good. But I want to go someplace new. See more of the country than just the northeast.

Damian is turning the car into an underground parking area. The garage is dark and stuffy. Not unexpected but I am ready to get out of it. Underground garages creep my out all by themselves but when you know there are vampires upstairs, bump the creep factor up to a million. Damian comes around the car pinning an I.D. card to his shirt. When he gets over to me, he checks my bag again just to be sure I have everything. I think it is more out of nerves than a need to make sure I have everything. "Damian! It's okay," I say lowering the bag. He leans his forehead against mine and takes a deep breath.

"I know but the thought of you going in there and getting hurt, or worse." He takes another deep breath before he continues, "Okay, Cornelius is on the top floor." Damian takes my hand and leads me to a door on the side wall. I don't know what I was expecting but stairs and another door into an office was not it. For some reason knowing that this is a vampire owned company, had me thinking more luxurious interior than concrete and stairs. We turn to the stairs and begin the climb. Up and up more stairs, and more. Good lord, enough with the stairs. Damian stops on the third landing and laughs at the look on my face as I look up to the fourth flight.

"Have vampires ever heard of elevators?" I say dryly.

"It's only two more flights," he says with a smile and a shake of his head.

"Yeah, says the vampire with great stamina. I, on the other hand, am a teenage girl who enjoys elevators." He laughs at my exaggerated voice. Damian then picks me up by the waist and sets me on the second step facing him. He then turns his back to me. I don't need to be told what to do; I take the chance to not have to climb any more stairs even though I very easily could have. I am in shape after all but I don't have to tell him that and ruin a free ride. I jump on his back and wrap my legs around his waist, hooking my ankles. He turns and starts up the stairs as if my added weight has no effect on him.

When we get to the fifth and last landing, he pauses looking over his shoulder at me. "Do I have to? I like it up here," I say placing a kiss to his cheek. He smiles shaking his head.

"Yeah, you have to, even though I do like you right there where I know you are safe." I climb down and straighten my clothes. I check to make sure my bag is good, that nothing fell out when I jumped on his back, then look to Damian. "I thought you said the bag was good?" he says with a knowing smirk. I once again go back to the five-year-old, and stick out my tongue.

He comes over to me and places his hands in my hair. Leaning his forehead on mine, he takes a deep breath of me. That seems to calm him. To be honest, it calms me as well. Opening his newly blue and green swirled eyes, he says to me, "No matter what, I love you and regret nothing. Okay?" For some reason that sounds so final. I do not care what I have to do, this is not going to be the final chapter for us.

"I love you, too," I say going on my tippy toes and using my grip on his side to kiss him. Just one simple kiss and I feel like I can take on the world. We break apart but don't let go for a moment.

With one more breath, he turns to the door with his hand in mine and pulls it open. Now this is what I expected a vampire company to look like.

Chapter 13

The carpet is a plush cream and the walls a deep red. We walk into a hall lined with large oak doors. The hall leads into an open area, which turns out to be a reception area. There is a big set of double doors directly in front of the hall and behind a desk with a pretty blonde. She looks up when we walk into the area and smiles at Damian, straightening herself out and pushing her generous chest out at him. Really, lady? "Damian! How good to see you!" She has on a big smile that clearly spoke of her interest in him. When she sees me on his hand, her smile turns into a sneer that clearly spoke of her utter and instant dislike of me. Which of course has me smiling sweetly at her. That makes her eyes burn.

"Hello, Claire, is he ready for us?" Damian asks, clearly oblivious of everything. Men.

"Yes. He is waiting for you, Damian" She could have at least attempted to hide her exclusion of me. Jeez, not so warm and fuzzy feelings in here.

"She seems nice," I whisper with sarcasm dripping off my tongue. We walk over to the double doors. When he pauses with his hand on the door, he looks down at me; I smile and squeeze his hand.

"You are nervous to bring me to meet your parents but here you are fine?" he asks laughing. "I told you that you are stronger than you think." He is right, for some reason I am fine.

Then again, *"I decided that I am going to take whatever is thrown at me. I'm a witch, dammit. I am the other, better—"* that makes him laugh *"—half of a vampire. Together we can do anything, overcome anything. I have faith. Okay, more like hope, that everything is going to be okay. I have to."* He squeezes my hand.

"Thank you, I needed to hear that."

"Anytime, fang boy."

"One last thing, Serena. Do me a favor."

"Anything, name it."

"Don't tell or let anyone find out that we can do this."

"You mean talk mind to mind? Why?"

"Because it may save us in the end. Either way, any advantage can't hurt."

With a smile, he pushes the door open saying, *"My evil little, witch."* This mind-to mind thing really does come in handy.

The office looks like an extension of the reception area. But in here there is a black leather couch to the left in front of a wall of books. Then on the right there is another leather couch and two leather chairs around a glass coffee table, all sitting in front of what looks like a mini bar. But what really catches your eye is the giant red maple desk in the middle of the room with a leather wingback chair, currently vacated. The man who occupies that chair is standing in front of the big picture window on the back wall. He is looking out of the window, seeming to not even notice our entrance. No one speaks.

I take the chance to really look at Cornelius Gray. To be honest, I was expecting a wrinkly old man. In reality, he is tall, though not as tall as Damian, maybe six foot. His build is muscular with wide shoulders and lean legs. He is obviously a warrior; if the weapons on the wall doesn't tell you that, the build of the man will. I wonder how old he is? Damian says he is really, really old but now I wonder just how old?

Before I can even blink, he is standing directly in front of Damian. Ice blonde hair, cut short, and nearly black eyes; Cornelius is contrast personified. "A witch, Damian? You know better," is all he says before he turns and walks around his desk to sit in his chair. "Okay, Damian, explain. I know that you would not think to break a law you helped put in place." Damian walks over to stand in front on the desk, bringing me with him.

"Serena is my soul mate and before you say anything just let us explain, Please." Cornelius looks like he is about to rebuke that. "Please, Cornelius." He looks at me and I can see the disbelief in his eyes. But when he looks back to Damian, they soften. He really does care for him and it is because of that, I am sure, that he nods. Damian takes a deep breath before he begins our story.

"Two nights ago. I woke from a dead sleep with an extreme need to get in my car and drive. I didn't though, I fought it, tossing and turning all night till I finally gave up. I had no idea why I was going or where. I just went with it. I found myself parking my car in a high school parking lot in a small town 20 minutes from here. I sat there willing myself to turn around and go home, but I couldn't. By noon I gave up and went inside and asked for a tour. I told them it was because I was considering transferring.

"I walked out of the office and started down the hall with the guidance counselor when I saw her," Damian squeezes my hand and looks at me, "in the window. In that moment, I didn't care why I was there, I was glad that I was. I ended up signing up for classes and was standing in the parking lot waiting for the bell to ring so I could hopefully see her again. I knew she was a witch, Cornelius. I just didn't care, I had to see her. I ended up following her home. I sat down the road from her house until I was finally able to pull myself away. I waited in the parking lot yesterday morning till she got there. When I started walking to her, I felt it. It felt like a stretched-out rubber band that was finally coming back together, that is the only way to explain it. It was pulling me to her. I had to fight not to run just so I could get to her sooner."

So he had felt all of that too, good to know. "Then when I touched her, the world shook. I thought that it couldn't get any stranger than that, but when she turned around and looked into my eyes, that rubber band snapped and wrapped around us, turning to steel. After that, I had no desire, no strength, to ever walk away from her." He turns to me, "I have been waiting almost 500 years for her." I smile at the utter and all-consuming love that is in his eyes, knowing they are reflected in my own.

I turn to Cornelius to see him watching Damian. "My grandmother, Elizabeth Rae, and her husband cast a spell that future generations would find their soul mates or really that their soul mate would find them when their powers are awakened on their 18th birthday. That is why Damian had an uncontrollable need to come to me. The spell was so powerful that it killed them both. I don't think that he could have ever fought it."

Cornelius sits silent for a moment looking from one of us to the other. I can see the disbelief in his eyes. Until he really looks at us, or more at our eyes. He gives his head a shake and ignores it. "How do I know that what you speak is the truth? I can see the love between you, and that your eyes seem to match now, but how do I know that this isn't just infatuation and contact lenses?" Cornelius leans forward placing his elbows on the desk and his chin on his entwined fingers as he looks to Damian. "But you already know what I am going to do to solve that, don't you?" Then he does something I didn't see coming, he smiles. "Yes, well, I trained you to think like me, didn't I?" He stands and walks around the desk. "Well, come then, let's get this over with."

Cornelius comes and stands in front of me. "Hello, I am Cornelius Gray, sire to Damian Drake and Grand Master of the North American Vampire Council."

That seems a little formal but okay. "Hello, I am Serena Rae, soul mate to Damian Drake and witch extraordinaire. And yes, that is my official title if anyone asks," I say shaking the hand he holds out to me. That makes Cornelius laugh and oddly enough it sounds natural. Cornelius is tough and more than capable to kill, but I am beginning to believe a little nice as well, in a deadly Vampire master kind of way.

"Oh, I do like her, Damian, I truly hope what you say is true because I would hate for her to die in that room." That puts a damper on things.

"Way to kill the mood," I say as Damian says, "She could kill me too, Cornelius."

Cornelius walks back to his desk and pushes a button and begins speaking to Claire. I'm not listening though. I give Damian a look that says how much I do not appreciate that statement. "Not that you would or will," he says when he sees it, "just that you could." I roll my eyes at him.

"Okay, love birds, let's go," Cornelius says as he walks around us; apparently, he has not missed our still joined hands. He leads us to a wall in the office that turns out to be an elevator.

I look up at Damian. "I never said that we had no elevators." He doesn't give me the chance to say anything but instead pulls me into the elevator as soon as the doors open.

"A meal will be brought to you three times a day, Serena dear," Cornelius says as the doors close and the elevator starts its descent.

"Ha, it took you a day to get a dear and me," I say grabbing his wrist to see his watch, "thirty minutes," I finish triumphantly. It's the little things in life really. "Give me a week and I'll be up to princess."

Damian looks over to Cornelius. "Thanks," he says dryly.

"No problem, I do what I can. Though she is probably right. I really do like her, she will be up to princess rather quickly," he says looking serious, surprising me, though I can see the mirth in his eyes.

"Don't encourage her, Cornelius!" Damian cries as we get off the elevator, I can't help but laugh.

We walk into a hall lined with rather strong looking doors each with a small window. Cornelius leads us to the last door on the right; opening it, he moves out of the way. I move to go into the room but am pulled up short when Damian stops. "Can you make sure her parents have some way to get a hold of her?" he asks. I had completely forgotten about that; good thing Damian is thinking.

"Of course. I will check on you sporadically, my son. Good luck to you both." With that Damian walks into the room and the door is shut with a finalized slide of the lock.

Chapter 14

Friday, Day One

"That went well," I say looking around my new temporary home.

"Oh and, Serena," I turn to see Cornelius in the window, "no feeding, Damian. If you do, I will be forced to kill you both, and I do not want to do that," he says as a matter of fact and nothing more. Great, well, there goes that idea I hadn't even known I had.

So…back to looking around. It is a fairly big room with a bed that sits in the far-right corner. It is on the floor covered in warm looking blankets in a deep purple. I laugh. An area rug covered in pillows lays next to the wall nearer the door. A stack of books sits on the carpet against the wall as well. On the opposite wall, a curtain hangs; I walk over to see that the curtain hides a bathroom. I hadn't even thought of the bathroom situation, at least we can have a little privacy.

"Not all the rooms are like this. They all have beds and books, but Cornelius had someone bring in the blankets and rug and curtain. I think he wanted us to be a little more comfortable. Or more for you to be, nothing is going to make this any easier for me. Which is why they don't usually have more than a bed in here," he says coming up behind me and wrapping me in his arms.

"When will the pain start?" I ask, not wanting to know but needing to.

"By tomorrow morning, I will be cramping. By Sunday, it will feel like acid rolling in my stomach. And then progressively get worse. Normally I can fight the urge to bite for maybe three days. I have never gone more than that though."

Today is Friday, I didn't tell Sam that I wouldn't be in school. Focus, Serena. So in two days, Damian will be in serious pain. I don't like that. Not one bit. Okay, what to do first. I lean back into Damian.

"I didn't know there would be a shower; do you think I could get some clothes?" I ask, seeing Damian's clothes stacked in the bathroom. "It would be nice to change my clothes and not just my underwear. Wait! You knew that there would be a shower, why didn't you have me bring some clothes?"

Damian laughs pulling me back as he starts walking backwards to the bed. "I thought we could use it as an excuse to see your parents one last time. We can ask when lunch is brought down since it is past noon. Wouldn't want to starve the powerful witch," he says bringing us crashing to the bed sideways. I land laughing.

"Lunch just for me or for you too?" I ask, turning so I can see him. He leans up on his elbow looking down at me.

"Both of us probably," he says, running the back of his knuckles down my cheek causing me to close my eyes. I feel his eyes travel across me. "This is going to be harder than I thought," he growls, then the cold seeps in. Before I open my eyes, I know he is gone. I don't even bother sitting up to look for him, I know where he is and why he is there. Damian has more than one urge to battle being locked in this room with me and if I don't control my own urges, he won't be able to control his. Now I am no virgin, it's the 21st century after all, but Damian is old fashioned and I can understand that. Truth be told, I like that, I want to wait too. After all, 24 hours is not a long time to know someone, no matter how it feels. So I sit up and move to lean against the wall and wait for him to calm down and return to me. With any luck, I will have my own hormones calm by then.

"Why no bed frame, or really any piece of furniture?" I ask looking over to Damian leaning against the door.

He looks over to me. "Because they could be used as a weapon. When a vampire gets locked in these rooms, it is for one of two reasons: either he is being tested for his loyalty, so he can work here, or he is a prisoner and we need information. Either way, furniture can be made into a weapon to kill yourself when the pain becomes unbearable." He started walking back to me while talking, then climbs on the bed and sits next to me, taking my hand. His feet reach over the bed and I laugh, resting my head on his shoulder. "What's funny?"

"You're tall."

"Why is that funny?" he asks in a bemused voice after a moment.

"I don't know."

Damian chuckles. "Now that is funny."

"And so begins our time in lockup." I sigh and Damian laughs harder.

We sit there just talking about this and that until the door unlocks and a big burly man that looks more like a giant comes in. Seriously, he has to duck to go through the door. He must be six seven at least and nothing but muscle. I look up at him as he sets down the tray of food he is carrying on the bed. I hear Damian laughing but can't tell why, then I feel his hand on my chin, lifting it up. I snap out of it and look over at him. "I didn't want flies to get in and choke you," he laughs, trying his hardest to be serious and failing miserably.

"All laughs until that actually happens," I say, then turn to thank the giant, or is it giant vampire, or vampire giant?

"As if I would let a fly hurt you." That makes me laugh. The mammoth leaves without saying a word.

"Well, he was chatty. Are all vampires like that? I don't even think he smiled."

"Danny is…modest. People see his size and that is all they take from him. No one thinks to listen to how smart he is, or how kind he is. So he doesn't talk and he keeps to himself."

"That is so sad and so mean," I say, watching the door until Damian puts a turkey sandwich under my nose and my stomach growls. Okay, fine, I'll eat then contemplate how to get Danny the Giant to smile. Why I want to so bad, I don't know but I will get him to smile, dammit. "So do you think everyone knows what is going on? Why you are locked in here with a witch, I mean?" I ask.

"Oh, I'm sure. Cornelius would have let the Council know immediately. I can guarantee that they are not happy about his choice to just lock me in this room with you."

"Why?"

"Most have wanted me dead for a long time. The fact that I have now broken a law that should see me dead but has not, will infuriate them. In the end, there is nothing they can do, Cornelius is the law and his decision is final."

"Okay, why have most wanted you dead? I feel as though this is something I should know." Damian actually laughs. "This is not funny, I don't like someone wanting you dead."

"You have nothing to worry about. The members of the council have known for some time that Cornelius plans for me to take over. They do not like that their chances for killing Cornelius are much lower. None of them are strong enough yet and have been biding their time. With me getting stronger and being personally trained to take on Cornelius, none of them have a chance at winning against either of us." He is silent for a minute eating his sandwich. When we are both done, he looks at me. "I would be surprised if Bernard is not already dead for trying to kill Cornelius for allowing this. He has been the most open about not liking me. I was planning to kill him as soon as I took over, if he is still alive to see that."

"Do you think that's part of the reason Cornelius didn't kill you, or me really, is because he realizes that with me by your side you can take over sooner? And why does he want to die so bad anyway? There has got to be something worth living for," I ask, beginning to get curious.

"I think that is part of why he didn't. Cornelius is one of those people that have a hard outer shell he uses to protect his people, but really he is a marshmallow inside. I think he also saw the love between us. He would have not even acknowledged that you were with me if he hadn't. As for him being adamant about me taking over, you try living as long as he has alone. Life is only worth living if you have people around who truly love and care for you. Cornelius has me, but...he is alone. And has been for...well, ever."

Really, there are no words for that other than I am glad I was not eating or drinking anything while I learnt that bit of information.

"When you live for so long alone, you can either become bitter or understanding that love is more important than anything else. Cornelius once told me that he would give up all the power in the world to have love." That is what I picked up on with Cornelius, envy. "I think he has started to feel the loneliness more and more over the centuries. I am the closest thing to family he has." Damian goes silent for a second, thinking. "He would never purposely take love from anyone but he also would never risk it not being real and possibly cause a problem for our secrecy or even the witches' secrecy. Hence the test to see that it is real."

"I hope he finds someone one day," I say snuggling up to Damian.

"So do I," he says kissing my hair. "If for no other reason than I don't have to kill him. Cornelius has become a father to me and I don't want to fight him, or even take over as Grand Master. But I will if that is what he wants."

"You don't want to be Grand Master?"

"Hell no. To deal with all the whining and power plays all the time, just watching from the back is tiring. I owe Cornelius my life and I will do it for him, but if I had any other choice... no, I don't want to be Grand Master."

I sit up and look at him. He is serious. I thought that is what he wanted, but he is serious. Damian Drake, the successor to Cornelius Gray, does not want to be Grand Master of the Vampire Council. He would make an amazing Grand Master and I was willing to help him achieve that but, "We will find a way for you not to have to do it then. Oh, I know! We can find a woman for Cornelius," I say as I lay back on his shoulder.

He laughs at me saying, "That should go over well with him." I smile. I will travel the whole world looking for a woman for Cornelius if it means Damian doesn't have to fight him and become Grand Master when he doesn't want to.

"You want to see something?" I ask to change the subject. I know that there are still so many questions that need to be answered. Like how he owes Cornelius his life. I know that Cornelius was the one to change him, but…that is a topic for another time. I rather keep the mood high on our first day in here. I wipe the crumbs off my hands and I hold my arm out. I watch as the blue and green swirl that is my power form in my hand simply by imagining it traveling through me. I take Damian's hand and I give him the ball, letting my power pass into his palm so he can hold the orb with me. I can feel the heat, the flames that lick the outside of the orb, my power. But I am not scared of it burning either of us, because it is us.

"Amazing! How are you doing that? How am I able to hold it?" Damian doesn't take his eyes off the ball in his palm. I watch him watch it and I know the answer.

"Because we are one, we are two souls together. This power, my power, is us. I figured it out last night in a dream. We are one soul. My power is your power."

Chapter 15

Damian looks down at me, a small smile tugging at his lips. "Forever," he says closing his palm, causing the orb to disappear. He brings his palm up to rest on my cheek as he leans the rest of the way down and closes his lips on mine. It doesn't go any farther than that. He pulls back and looks to the corner of the room. I turn to look and for the first time I see the camera. Huh, how did I miss that earlier? Well, that should help keep us from doing anything more. I look to Damian. Maybe.

He turns back to me and before his lips can find mine again, there is a knock at the door. His forehead drops to mine as he breathes out in frustration. No sooner has he done that than, he slides across the bed so we can just hold hands. "It's okay, Cornelius, let them in."

"Let who in?" The door opens to let in Cornelius and behind him, my parents. I so did not see that coming.

"Mom! Dad!" I get off the bed and run to them.

"Oh, honey! How are you?"

"Fine, Mom. I have only been gone four hours. What are you doing here? How did you even know where here was?" I turn to Damian. "We completely forgot to ask for clothes for me when Danny came in earlier."

"No, we didn't, Danny overheard us talking about it."
Oh right, vampires.

"Cornelius called and asked if we could bring you some clothes." I turn and smile at him.

"Anything for you, princess," he says which brings a groan from the bed.

"You said that on purpose. Nearly five hundred years you have known me, Cornelius, and you side with her? That's cold."

"But it got her to smile and knowing she will rub it in just makes it even better," Cornelius says with a shrug.

"Told you I would get to princess," I turn and say to Damian.

"That does not count," he counters. I just laugh and turn back to my parents to see them looking confused. I shake my head and take the bag from my dad's hand.

"Thank you," I say looking through it as I walk to the bathroom. I hear my mom ask Damian what that was all about. I smile waiting for him to answer.

Walking back out, I hear him say that it is a long story. "No, it's not. He said he would get you to call him slugger by the end of the week, I said I would get Cornelius to call me princess by the end of the week. I win!"

"Doesn't count!" he says getting off the bed and coming over to me, wrapping his arms around my waist.

I look over to Cornelius. "Verdict?" I ask.

"He can't give a verdict, he has already shown bias."

"It counts," Cornelius says with a smile. I laugh when Damian looks at him mouth agape.

"Cold, Cornelius, cold."

"What can I say, I'm loveable," I say with all innocence.

"Yes, you are, my evil little witch," Damian says, leaning over to kiss me.

Cornelius shakes his head and walks out saying, "I will give you a minute with your parents, but no more."

"Thank you," my parents say together.

"Serena, why don't you show them what you just showed me," Damian says, holding out his palm. I smile and instead of making the ball and handing it to him, I place my palm under his and make the ball right into his hand.

When my parents first explained that I am a witch, two days ago – damn it feels like forever ago – I didn't think it would come this easy. I only have to feel what I want to do. To picture it coming to life in front of me. With Damian by my side, it is easier. I don't know why, and really, I don't care.

To know that I never have to feel alone, that I never again will feel that I am missing something, is amazing. That knowledge helps me to know what I have to do, to know who I am, and what I *can* do.

I feel the power within me and I push it down my arm and through my hand, right into Damian's palm. I look up and smile at him. "You are getting better and better at that," he says to me with a big smile.

I look over at my parents. "Serena, you continue to astound me. We are so proud of you."

"Thanks, Mom," I say as I let the power flow back into me. I walk over to them and give them each a hug.

"Cornelius said we can call and talk to you for the next couple of days but when Damian starts to feel... not so good, it would be best if we were to let you two be."

"He's right, it will be best for Serena to not have any distractions."

"You won't hurt me, Damian," I say with absolute certainty.

"Still better to be safe than sorry, Serena. I want you to be focused in case you have to take action."

"It's okay, Seri, we will talk to you when it's over. Cornelius will let us know." Apparently, they have talked quite a bit with Cornelius. They give me a hug together. "We love you," they say as one. My mom walks over to Damian and gives him a hug. Then something I didn't think I would ever see, happens; my dad walks over and grabs Damian into a hug and slaps his back saying, "Take care of my baby."

"Always," Damian answers.

I shake my head and walk over to Damian. "Is the love-fest over?" I ask as Damian pulls me to stand in front of him and hangs his arms over my shoulders.

"You're just jealous because I got a hug," he says and my parents laugh. I look over at them.

"Oh, you two did that on purpose!" I accuse and they laugh harder.

Walking to the door my mom says, "Well, it is only fair since Cornelius does seem a bit biased."

"My own parents! My flesh and blood!" They smile as they walk out of the room. The door closes behind them and my mom looks in the window and blows a kiss before walking away.

I turn to Damian to see him smiling. If he didn't look so cute, I would slap him. I shake my head and walk over to the corner to look at the books. I sit on my knees and read some of the titles. "You have got to be kidding me! Twilight, Dracula, The Vampire Diaries?" I look over at Damian who is trying very hard not to laugh.

"I think those are for your reading benefit. A joke from Cornelius." Then he lost it.

"That's nice, lock me in a room with a vampire and give me vampire books to read. Funny, unfortunately I don't think any of these will help me much," I laugh, "But thanks."

Damian sobers up and crosses the room to me. "That's right, because anything you want to know, all you have to do is ask," he says as he sits next to me. "Oh, look, this one isn't a vampire book." He grabs a book and shows me the cover.

"In Cold Blood, really? Is that supposed to make me feel better?" I say shaking my head. He sets the book back on the stack and turns my face to look at him with his hand on the cheek. For a minute, all he does is stare into my eyes while rubbing his thumb along my cheek. I still cannot get over the new color of his eyes and to know that mine look the same. Amazing and beautiful. But I do miss the ocean blue swirl that I first looked into.

"We will be okay," he whispers. I grab his hand and turn my head to kiss his palm.

"I know we will, but you are going to be in so much pain and I don't like that," I say, keeping my lips on his palm and breathing deeply, I love the smell of his skin. I feel a shiver run up his arm and smile.

"Not funny," he says, his voice husky and deep. Then he's gone.

"Can I ask you a question? Why is it so much harder for you to be near me here than it was at my parents' house?" I ask as I turn back to the books and give him a minute.

I can feel the smile in is voice as he says, "Because I knew that your parents were right down the hall. Here, there is no one to slap me… or shoot me." I laugh at that. I figured as much but still had to ask.

I turn to look at him, needing to see his reaction. "What if I promise to slap you? Will you stop running to the other side of the room?" To that he gives me a droll stare that clearly says how much he believes I will stop him. I laugh, he's right. As soon as his lips touch mine, I lose all brain function. "Okay, so maybe not, but I really wish you would stop running, I feel very cold when you leave my side."

Damian crosses the room back to me and holds out his hand to take mine. When my hand is safely clasped in his, he pulls me up with so much force that our bodies touch everywhere and my feet are off the floor. "Is that warm enough?" I lose the skill needed to speak as he allows me to slide down to the floor. All I can do is nod, and he smiles, which then leads to my not being able to breath. He really is too damn sexy for my own health.

When my feet touch the floor, I push away from him far enough that I can keep my hands on his forearms but close my eyes and lean down to catch my breath, using his arms to keep me standing. Crap, this is going to be hard. When I can breathe again, I open my eyes and start to rise.

"Okay, you are right, running is good," I say breathless. But instead of running, his hands tighten on my arm. That gets me to look into his eyes only to have my heart begin to hammer out of my chest. Damian's eyes are glowing, well no, just the green in his eyes is glowing, how strange. My face must have given away to something being weird.

"What's wrong?" he asks and the green begins to fade back to the normal swirl mixed with blue. For a second I thought that the blue was completely gone.

"The green in your eyes was glowing to the point that the blue was almost unseen," I answer, taking my hands off his arms and putting them on his cheeks to bring his head closer and look into his eyes. They are back to normal now. "Was mine doing to same thing?" I ask pulling back.

"Honestly, I don't know, when you looked up, my eyes were locked on your lips because all I could think was how much I wanted to kiss you. I only looked up to your eyes when your lips went from 'kiss me' to 'what the hell,'" he says and I laugh. Good grief, apparently, he doesn't even need to look me in the eyes to know what I am thinking. I slap his arm when I catch him looking back at my lips. "What? I love how expressive your lips are without you even having to speak," he says smiling. And I am lost. With my hand that is still on his cheek, I shift it to the nape of his neck and pull him down to me.

I kiss him with all the love, all the passion, all of my heart. He fists my hair in his hands and pulls me closer to the point that we are one. There is no space between us. No air can slip through us, yet it still is not close enough. If I don't stop this, I will rip all of the clothes off him. I want nothing more in the world than to feel his skin against mine. I love the feel of his arms around me. Being wrapped in his arms makes me feel safe and at home. I was made to be right here in this vampire's arms.

Damian's hands leave my hair and move down my back, causing tremors to travel all through me. To that he growls deep in his throat, which causes shivers to run down my spine. Damian moves his hands to my waist and starts to push away. I know he is right to do it, we need to stop, but I cannot control my magic even if I wanted to at this moment. My power reaches out and pulls him back to me as if I have extra hands. I pull back to smile at him. Then I see his eyes. They are once again bright swirling green.

He lifts me up and turns us around walking to the bed. Without taking his hands off my back to catch us before hitting the mattress that is sitting on the floor, he drops, trusting me to make sure we land softly. Without even thinking about it, I slow down our descent and set us softly on the bed.

"Good job," he says, sounding breathless even in my head; I smile against his lips. He kisses me one last time before moving his lips across my cheek and down to my neck, making me moan. He nips my neck above the artery, causing electricity to run down to my toes and my eyes to pop open, landing on the camera in the corner. *Crap, talk about a buzzkill!* I unwrap my ankles leaving my knees against his hips and push with my arms to roll him. Catching him by surprise, he rolls over without a problem, leaving me on top of him. Then with all of my self-control and with a whole lot of regret, I push myself off of him and up to the top of the opposite wall. I don't allow myself to drop to the floor yet not trusting that I won't run back to him, cameras be damned.

Chapter 16

Damian is flat on his back on the bed with his arms stretched out looking at me. His breathing just as heavy as mine. *"Cameras,"* I send to him. He doesn't turn his head but his eyes dart over to them. Then back to me.

"I'm sorry," he says.

"Why? This was all me, you tried to pull away but I wouldn't let you, didn't want you to."

"That was impressive by the way. It felt like two more pairs of arms encircled me and pulled me in. I don't even think I could have fought if I had wanted to. It was that strong."

"You didn't want to fight it?" I ask, smiling at him. He gives me a 'duh' stare, his eyes back to the blue and green swirl. Interesting. *"So, did my eyes do the same thing?"*

"Yes, they did, but not with the green, the blue brightened up and looked like it was taking over. I have a theory if you would like to come down from the ceiling."

"I'm not on the ceiling, I'm on the wall."

Damian laughs while he sits up. He switches to speaking since our breathing has somewhat slowed down and says, "You might as well be on the ceiling, your head is bumping against it. When you flew up there, I thought I was going to have a heart attack. I thought you were going to whack your head."

I give an undignified snort as I float back down and across the room. Lifting my legs up, I lower myself onto the bed to sit next to him. Immediately, he takes my hand and begins to rub his thumb over my knuckles. I close my eyes and lean my head against the wall. Oh, how I love him! After a few minutes of silence, I open my eyes to find him staring at me with a small smile. "What?"

With his free hand, he pulls me to him and gives me the most tender and loving kiss I have ever experienced. It is a small, short kiss but left me more breathless than an hour's make-out session could have. He pulls back just enough to place his forehead against mine and stares deep into my eyes. "I love you."

"Prove it," I say joking with him.

"How would you like me to do that?" he asks smiling.

"Scream it to the world." He leans over and whispers I love you to me. "That was the worst scream ever." I laugh.

"Well, I didn't want to hurt you by screaming in your ear." He laughs.

"I told you to scream to the world."

"You are my world."

I am silent for a moment as I look at him staring down at our joined hands. "Oh, that was smooth. Totally cheesy, but sweet." I laugh while my cheeks turn bright red. *"I love you, Damian. You really are a prince charming, aren't you? That was the sweetest thing ever."*

He smiles. "I love you, too."

We sit not speaking for a while. Finally, I can't take it in anymore. If we do not put a little distance between us, I am going to jump him again. *"Okay, Damian, get my head out of the gutter, what is your theory?"* I say leaning away from him.

"Well, that is not going to get your head out of the gutter, but possibly put it further in." Great. I slide further away.

"Okay, go ahead." Damian laughs as he leans against the wall and closes his eyes.

"Okay, well, even before this, I have been thinking about what had happened in that orb. Somehow your magic changed both of us on a genetic level. To be honest, I don't think it was just your magic. I don't think just in the eyes neither. I think we merged. Two souls became one, two power sources or energy sources became one. There are times when I swear I feel your power in me. I wrote it off as the love I feel for you growing. But when you pulled me back to you earlier, that felt like vampire strength, not just magic.

"As for the eyes glowing, I think whenever either of us gets turned on, our eyes glow. I'm wanting you so the green that was originally your color glows brighter, and vice versa." He opens his eyes and looks at his hands. "I think that in that orb, while we were kissing, we literally became two halves of one whole. I think you may have some vampire traits and I some witch traits." He pauses. "I have never heard of a witch being able to pull with vampire strength even using magic, or a vampire being able to hold a witch's fire or power orb." He pauses again. This time he looks at me and I feel the weight of what he is about to say. "Which then makes me wonder if you are now immortal."

Damian reaches across the space that is between us and pulls me to him. Settling next to him with my head on his shoulder, I have to wonder if he is right. I know that I don't have heightened senses but can I use vampire strength with my magic? Could he be right? Could more have changed in that orb than just our eye color? *Am* I now immortal? Do I have to worry about growing old and dying? I don't want to ever leave Damian and the thought of making him watch me wither and die breaks my heart. "I hope I am immortal. We haven't talked about that yet. What are we going to do if I'm not? I don't want you to have to watch me die."

"Don't worry, love, I wouldn't." I stop him there, knowing what he is going to say.

"To think of a world without you in it just doesn't seem right. So don't even say it, Damian. Let's just hope I am immortal."

All of this talk of dying is too depressing, so why not test if I do have the strength of a vampire? I scoot across the bed and stand up. Looking to Damian, I smile at his perplexed look. "Stand up on the other side please," I tell him. Not questioning why, he stands on the other side of the bed. "Okay, now I want you to fight it, okay?" And even though he looks nervous and a bit confused, he nods, *Goddess, I love him.*

I reach out to him with invincible arms and pull. Immediately, he plants his feet and leans back, not allowing me to bring him across the bed. I close my eyes and look inside myself, searching for any power that was not there before, not really expecting to find anything. After all, I am new at this and don't yet know my limits. I can see the source of my power, the orb that contains all that is good and pure inside of me. My love, and my passion. So I dive deeper into it. I don't have to look very far before I find what I am looking for.

The center of my power is Damian. He is right. What was originally a green swirl of power is now a swirl of green and blue, and it holds more than I thought. The blue is not just him. What I didn't know before, what I had not considered, is that the blue is his power. We had begun to merge before the orb, it started the moment he touched me. But it all changed when he was pulled into the power orb with me.

With a smile so big, I think I might break, I give a tug of my new-found strength and bring him to me as I open my eyes. I wrap my entire self around him and kiss him so fully that neither of us can breathe. When I pull back, I smile at him and say, "I found it."

Damian laughs. "I guess so."

"You are right, we did merge. I do have your strength. More than that, Damian. With time I will figure out what all I have of yours but I think that even now we are entangled."

"Yes, we are, Serena, very good," he says to me, looking at our entangled bodies with such mirth and sarcasm I smack his arm.

"Not that, smart ass."

He laughs. "You found what?"

"I knew from the beginning that the blue was you. Not just because it is, or was, the color of your eyes, but because it was emanating from you. I didn't look closer until now. I didn't think about looking closer until now. It is your energy. Your essence."

He is quiet for a moment, thinking. I can tell that what I said struck something in him. He has come up with a new theory.

We stand there just holding each other until the door to the cell opens and Silent the Giant comes in with a tray of food. *Silent the Giant! Perfect.* I look over to the clock on the wall to see that it is six already; damn, today went fast. Danny places the food on the bed and turns to leave.

"You know, Danny, if you keep bringing food for me, I may start to think you care." To my utter shock, Danny smiles, just a little lift of his lips, but a smile none-the-less.

"The food is for both of you, and it is part of my job," he answers, losing the smile and giving me a hard look.

"Holy shit, he smiles and talks, Damian, call the news crews!" To that Danny actually chuckles before closing the door. "I heard that! You're not dying, are you? Danny? You okay after the chuckle?"

To my surprise, he answers, "Yes I'm fine... thankfully."

"Oh my god, he spoke again and was that a joke!?" Damian, who had gone over to sit on the bed, starts to laugh.

"Eat, witch, before I take your food," Danny answers.

Walking over to sit next to Damian, I laugh. "I think I like him."

"I like you, too," Danny says in a soft voice before masking it with a hard, "Now eat." I giggle and look down at the plates; steak, broccoli, and mashed sweet potatoes. It all smells amazing. I cut off a piece of steak and take a bite, I can't help the moan that escapes, causing Damian to nearly choke when he starts to laugh.

"Sorry, but this is really good."

"I feel a little jealous that a steak can entice a moan like that out of you," he says and I laugh as I take another bite.

We talk about this and that while we eat. Mostly about Sam and me. Places that I want to see. Things that I want to do; turns out that there are a lot of things that Damian wants to do too. He is surprised by that as much as I am, I think.

"So have you been doing nothing but work for the last 464 years?" I ask.

"Pretty much, but that's okay, because now we can experience things together, first time for both of us." Damian sets the tray by the door and comes back over to the bed.

"So you will go sky diving with me? Canoeing? Horseback riding?"

"I have been horseback riding. Did it for a very long time, but if you want to, then yes." I smile at him.

"What about…taking a cooking class, or backpacking through Europe, or visiting the tea house on top of Mt. Hua in China, or learn to surf, or…"

"Okay, yes, we can do all of it, anything you want, Serena. We have forever." He laughs.

I hope we have forever. "You do realize that forever is a very long time, and that leaves me with a lot of time to figure out even more things to do."

"Yes, and I am so glad my life will never be boring with you. But can we focus on surviving the next week?"

"I guess," I answer laughing. Damian gets up and walks over to the books, looking through them. He comes back with one in his hands. Without showing me the book, he stacks the pillows up and lays down, waving me over. I lay resting my head on his chest. He shows me the book and I laugh.

"Romeo and Juliet seemed fitting."

As Damian reads to me, I lose the words and focus on the sound of his voice. So soothing, so calming. I love his voice and it amazes me that the first time I heard it, was less than two days ago. Even then I felt as though I have heard that voice all my life.

His voice is like melted dark chocolate that runs through me and makes my whole body shiver and feel utterly safe. Spending the rest of forever listening to him is something I will definitely be looking forward to.

To think that I didn't want this, that when my parents first told me about my soul mate, I was not happy. Why? What had I been so worried about? This relationship, this love, is not confining. I can still do all I want to and have someone do them all with me. Damian wants me to go to college, he wants me to see the world. What is more, he wants to do it all with me. It is sad to think that for how old he is, there is still so much that he has not been able to do, or just didn't want to. To know that meeting me has awakened him, and has made him want to truly live, fills me with so much joy.

As he reads, his accent becomes more prominent which makes me smile. Knowing that in a few days I will be hearing this sweet voice in pain, breaks my heart. I fist the hand on his chest, grabbing tight on his shirt. I hope that in some way, by some miracle, I can help him through this.

For now though, I can just enjoy having this. Relaxing and listening to his voice read me a story of forbidden love. Our ending will not be so tragic, I will make sure of that.

With a surge of power running through my body, I take comfort in the knowledge that we can take on the world together.

I close my eyes and take a deep breath of Damian's woodsy masculine scent and let it soothe me along with his voice before I let sleep take me.

Chapter 17

Saturday, Day 2

As I wake up, it takes me a minute to remember where I am and why. Strong arms surround me before I can sit up. Okay, I am fine with lounging here all day as long as those arms never leave my waist.

"Good morning," Damian says in my ear in a sleep filled voice that melts my bones and sends goosebumps up my arm. Damian chuckles before kissing my ear and enticing a moan out of me which then makes him chuckle more.

"Keep laughing. You won't be when I have to throw myself back up the wall and this time I may hit my head. Then you are going to feel really bad," I threaten.

"Okay, you win." He laughs before pulling away. I cannot not stop the disappointed whine that escapes my mouth even if I tried, which makes him laugh as he zips to the bathroom.

"In a hurry, fang boy?" I ask.

"Yes, my evil little witch, I would not have been able to stop myself from climbing back in that bed with you if I took my time coming in here."

"Now why is that, sweetie?" I send that thought to him in the sweetest voice I can muster in my head.

"I can just see you batting your eyes right now," he laughs, *"and you know just why that is. I am going to have to change your nickname to evil little vixen."* I hear the shower turn on and throw myself back on the bed with a groan. How could I not have thought about this? All that is separating me and my no doubt naked vampire, who is the most gorgeous man on earth in my eyes, is a curtain.

"If you would like to call me that every once in a while, I think I will be okay with that, but I do like evil little witch." Then in a serious voice I say, *"Or really, 'my evil little witch.' I like being yours."* 'My evil little witch' doesn't really sound like a term of endearment, but coming from him it is the most loving thing anyone has ever said to me.

"You will forever be my evil little witch. But if you keep up with the moans and shivers and whines when I leave your side. I will have no choice but to call you my evil little vixen." The shower turns off and I sit up and look to the bathroom.

"Okay, as long as I can keep torturing you, I am fine with that." I hear his musical laugh run through my head.

"I am sure you are. That is okay, I will torture you right back." I don't bother sending my laugh to him, instead I laugh out loud. When the curtain opens, I look towards it. Turns out he wasn't kidding about torturing me. My breath roars out of me and my heart tries to beat out of my chest. Never in my life did I think the sight of a simple bare chest could cause me to lose all brain function. I was right about his shirt that first day I saw him; it did not leave anything to the imagination and I had every right to be jealous of a shirt.

Seriously; one, two, three, four, five, six, *seven, eight pack abs. I didn't even know that was possible*! My narrative voice is getting squeaky again, moving on. Defined pecks, wide muscular shoulders leading to muscular arms. All in perfect proportions that clearly showed he could hold his own, and that makes me want to kiss every inch of him. Crap, I am going to start drooling if I don't stop staring at him.

Now it is my turn to run. I get off the bed and run to the bathroom, making a wide circle around him. I hear him laugh as I close the curtain. *"Not nice, fang boy, not nice."* Actually, let me be honest, *"Okay, it is very nice . . . ugh fine, fan-frickin-tastic, but showing off your chest while I cannot touch you is not nice. Don't you dare laugh,"* I warn him. Usually I am not that honest, but this is Damian.

"I wouldn't dare laugh, and I wouldn't dare stop you from touching me either."

"I heard that laugh, fang boy!" I yell to his mind as I turn on the shower. I could torture him but I won't. That would torture me right back. This is going to be so much harder than I thought. Being locked in this room with him is torture in itself, in a very good way. Damn, but he has the most amazing chest.

I jump in the shower and quickly wash up, not wanting to be in here any longer than necessary. I dress and brush my teeth before opening the curtain and walk out with my hair brush.

"Aw, damn," Damian says in a whiny voice that surprises me.

"What?"

"I was really hoping you would come out with no shirt to get me back." I laugh as he grabs me in a hug. Pulling away, he takes the hair brush from me. Keeping my hand, he pulls me back to the bed and sits me down, turning me so my back is to him.

"This is the second time you have brushed my hair. Why?"

"Do you not want me to?" he asks sounding a little nervous.

"I actually love to have my hair brushed. I am just surprised. You do it without me even asking."

"I love the feel of your hair. Besides, it is just another way for me to touch you." I smile, then close my eyes and enjoy the feel of his hand in my hair following the brush's path.

"I'm sorry I fell asleep on you last night."

"Don't be, I know you were really tired." My stomach growls and Damian laughs as he gets up to take the brush to the bathroom. "They should be bringing in breakfast soon." Not ten seconds later, the door unlocks and Danny comes in.

"Danny!" I say in a happy chipper voice, that brings a smile out of him.

He quickly hides the smile before answering in a deadpan voice, "Serena." Meanwhile, Damian walks back to the bed, shaking his head and smiling at me.

"I promise you, Danny by the time all this is over, you will be so happy every time you see me that you will have to hug me. You know why? Because you are a stuffed-with-fluff giant teddy bear," I say in a baby talk voice.

"I'm a vampire, Serena," he says, giving me a stern, and what probably has caused others to shit their pants, look.

"Yes, yes you are. A giant vampire Pooh bear who wants to give me hugs." To that he lets his fangs out and hisses at me.

"Haven't we already clarified that you are indeed a vampire? Okay, fine, you can be a deadly vampire Pooh bear."

"That's better." Giving me a small smile, he turns and walks away, locking the door behind him.

"Why do you want him to give you a hug?" Damian asks while sitting down and getting settled.

"Because he needs a hug. I can tell," I say sitting on the other side of the tray.

"You are probably right. Are you going to find Danny a woman to?" he smiles.

"One train wreck at a time please."

The rest of the day goes by quickly. We talk, though not about anything important. I know that there is still a lot we need to learn about each other but to be honest, I don't want to do that here. Being locked in this room with possible doom leering over our heads is not the way I want to learn about his life. Besides, it would feel like we were getting all that stuff out before we die, crazy I know, but I would rather not feel like I had to know this stuff because we are getting ready to die, and would rather learn about him because I am getting ready to live.

So instead, we talk about Danny, and Cornelius, and Sam. We talk about the people in our lives. We talk more about our theory. We talk more about where we want to go. What we want to do. We finish Romeo and Juliet before

Danny brings in board games for us. I kick his hot ass at Scrabble. He beats me at Monopoly. Danny brings the phone in before lunch so I can talk to my parents. We don't talk very long before he comes back in for the phone, bringing with him our lunch.

I can tell that Damian is beginning to feel the cramps, but he never complains. The only way I can even tell is because every once and a while his hand will go to his stomach. Tomorrow it will be worse. I still do not know how I am going to deal with him in pain.

The rest of the afternoon flies by. Damian and I talk and play games. More than anything, we laugh.

At six, Danny comes in with our food. "You are so good to me, Danny!" He gives me a true smile. "I knew I would win you over at some point. I really thought it would be harder or at least take longer. But I am glad it didn't. You should smile more, Danny."

"Thank you, Serena." Danny looks over to Damian for the first time since being locked in this room yesterday morning. "I can see why you love her, she is truly special."

"Yes, she is," Damian says, looking at me with love filling his beautiful eyes.

I walk over to Danny before he can leave. "I knew you cared," I say giving him a hug.

"You'll do, Serena, you'll do," Danny says but does not return the hug. One step at a time. Danny locks the door while I walk back to Damian.

"I win."

"What are you talking about?"

"I promised myself yesterday when Danny brought us our lunch that I would get him to smile a real smile. I just did."

"So what do you win then," he asks.

I lean over the tray and kiss him. "Why would that be your prize when you can do that any time?"

"Because I love to kiss you. Any reason I can come up with, I will take it."

"Well, I can't argue with that," he says smiling.

After dinner, Damian lays on the bed while I pick a book to read to him. I walk over to the bed and before lying down show him the book, Dracula by Bram Stoker. I got a droll stare with an eye-roll. I consider it a victory and an okay, and lay down laughing. With Damian leaning against the wall, I lay with my head on his lap and he takes my hair and spreads in along his legs to begin running his hands through it. I close my eyes and savor his hands in my hair before starting.

At the end of chapter one, I look up to Damian to see him staring blankly at my hair with pain lines around his eyes and lips. "It is really starting to hurt, isn't it?" I ask.

He turns to look at me and lifts the corner of his lips in an attempted smile. Looking back at his hand in my hair, he says, "Yes, but nothing that I can't handle," then in a small voice that breaks my heart I hear him say, "yet." Looking back at me he takes the hand that is not in my hair and runs his knuckles along my cheek. "The longest I have gone without feeding is three days. Tomorrow's pain levels I have experienced before. It is after that that I am worried about. After tomorrow, you will want to keep your distance."

I grab the hand on my cheek and squeeze before bringing it to my lips and kissing each knuckle. "I will be fine. I am more worried about how much pain you will be in." Then before he can say anything, I start to read again. I know that he wants to argue, but there is no point. He won't hurt me so I'm not scared.

Damian takes his hand out of my hair but I pay no attention as I read, even though I immediately miss the feel of his soft touch in my hair. Then a light gleams over the book in my hands. I lean my head back into his legs to look. My mouth drops open when I see what is causing the extra light. I sit up and turn around to get a better look at the ball of fire in Damian's hand.

I look to Damian and see that he is just as shocked as I am. "I was curious to see what I got of you. I just did what you do, held my hand out and tried to search for the power inside, then bring it out. I was not expecting this though," he says looking to me with a mixture of shock and joy. I smile at him before turning back to the fire ball. I can feel the heat coming from it and reach out to see if it would burn me even though mine doesn't burn him. I grab the ball and oddly enough a piece breaks off in my hand.

"Cool." I close my hand picturing the ball burning out. I look to Damian to see him doing the same. "So you got my fire power. I wonder why that one and not levitation or something? It's because it is cooler, isn't it? Got to have the coolest power to show off, huh?" I say smiling.

"Duh," he says sounding just like a five-year-old talking to his parents who just figured out something that is so obvious to him but really makes no sense at all. I laugh at him. "No, it is probably because that was the first power that manifested in you," he says in a more serious voice.

"And I got your strength. I guess we will learn together if we get anything else." When he nods, I go on, "So can you search within and find another like you did the fire?"

"It isn't like that with me. You describe it like the magic in you is a living thing that you cannot only feel but see, right?" I nod. "Well, when I look inside to find the power, it is just extra energy that I feel. I just imagined it travelling to my hand. Kind of like making a kick more powerful. I cannot see it inside me like you can or feel it specifically like you can. I don't know how I will figure out what else I get, but I will eventually," he says with a smile. He pats his leg and I turn and lay back down. I open the book and continue reading while he puts his hand back in my hair and I can't help but sigh, only to hear his chuckle.

This, right here, is perfect. Even in this tiny room with concrete walls. Here with him running his hands through my hair while I read to him, is perfect. Tomorrow will come and the pain will increase but for right now, the world is good.

I'm not sure when, but my eyes just did not want to stay open and the words started to run together. At some point, Damian laughs and takes the book from me. I don't argue. I feel him move beneath me, then he picks me up and sets me down with my head on a pillow. Then blackness as I fall asleep.

Chapter 18

Sunday, Day 3

The next morning, I don't wake to Damian next to me. I open my eyes and look at the wall, turning my head to what appears to be an empty room. The shower isn't running. So where is he? I sit up and feel eyes on my back. Turning, I finally see him sitting in the corner. "Damian? Are you okay?"

"Yeah, I couldn't lay down anymore, but I didn't want to wake you by moving." His voice is strained, and every once and a while, I see his body shake. The pain has truly started.

"Is it really bad?"

"No, but that is because it isn't constant yet. I can still control the hunger but the control I have will slowly start to wane, that's when the pain will become constant."

I get up and walk over to him. His back is in the corner with his head leaning against the wall, knees up to his chest and arms resting on his bent knees; for all purposes, he looks relaxed. I know that it is so not the time, but my Goddess, is he gorgeous! I kneel down to him and he picks his head up to look at me. His face is relaxed so anyone looking at him would never know the pain he is in. But I'm not anyone, I can see the pain he is trying to hide loud and clear in his eyes.

"Oh Damian," I say cupping his face in my hands. He turns his head and kisses my palm.

"I'm okay, Serena, for now, so don't worry," he says taking my hands in his.

"I don't like seeing you in pain," he opens his mouth, "and don't you dare tell me to get used to it." He snaps his mouth closed.

"Well, you will have to for the time being."

"Fine, but you had better not make a habit out of this." He smiles at me, a real one that almost takes the pain out of his eyes. The lock slides open and Danny walks in with our breakfast.

"How are you feeling?" he asks Damian with what sounds like real sympathy and concern. I help Damian stand and we meet Danny.

"Peachy," Damian answers in a sarcastic voice. Danny laughs before turning to me.

"Be careful, never underestimate a hungry vampire," he warns before bending down to hug me, only to stop half way when Damian growls. I mean an actual growl. I lean over to see around Danny who had frozen completely. Damian is looking at Danny with death in his eyes. I have never seen Damian look this deadly and never want to again. Danny straightens without turning to look at Damian. "Sorry, old friend, she is yours." He smiles at me and then all but runs out of the room.

"What the hell was that for?" I ask with my hands on my hips. "I was about to get my hug!"

"I'm sorry. Vampires are possessive of what is ours. I don't like people touching you normally but I can control the urge to stop them. When I am like this, with my strength waning, I have a harder time controlling it."

"But he wasn't going to hurt me."

"I know, but still, someone touching you is enough to set me off when I am like this, and it will only get worse. Danny knows that, but just wasn't thinking or just didn't realize the amount of pain I am in and the lack of control from it," he says, sitting down to eat. He didn't look at me as he talked or when he sat.

"Damian," I say, waiting for him to look at me; I don't move, don't say anything more, just wait. Just when I think he isn't going to, he turns his head and looks up into my eyes. That is when I see it, he is embarrassed that he had lost control. Even for that little thing. He didn't hurt Danny, he just warned him not to touch me. "It's okay, I understand, and I am sure Danny doesn't blame you for growling at him."

"I know, I'm just not used to this possessiveness, I don't know how to handle it." He takes a deep breath that causes him to wince. "I have never been in love before, let alone consider someone mine." This isn't really news to me. He hasn't come out and said as much until now but I just knew that this was a first for him.

"Really? You have never been in love before? How can that be? You are *OLD!*"

I laugh at the look he gives me, and I see him smile, a real smile. "Thanks for that reminder, but no. I haven't really had time, ironically enough. Although this has happened fast, I don't think it would have with anyone else." He pats the bed, beckoning me to sit. When I do, he continues, "Like I said before, I have been training with Cornelius and working for the Council. Not much time to have a social life. Now that I think of it, I never had the urge to meet someone. I have always hated being alone and envied others who found love but I never… I don't know… needed to look for it. I guess deep down I knew that it would find me when the time was right."

"But you found me," I say smirking at him.

"Yes and no. I did come to you, but it was your power that brought me there."

Hmm, I guess he is right. "Okay so we found each other."

"That is right, my evil little witch. We are equals in all things."

"Why are you speaking in my mind?"

"Because by the end of the day, this is all I will be able to do."

"That is sad, Damian. Will you really be that bad by the end of the day?"

"Yes. Don't worry, Serena, I will be fine." Don't worry, don't worry, don't worry. He keeps saying that, as if that is possible.

"I love you, Damian. I will always worry, and I never want to see you in any pain."

"I love you too, Serena." He leans over the tray and kisses me briefly before pulling back. I can see that it had pained him to move.

We don't play any games today. He says that he will but I can see that he is tired, I don't think he got much sleep last night. Besides, I can tell he doesn't really want to. With

Damian in pain, he doesn't have the strength to do much of anything. He is able to take a shower after breakfast. When he is done, he comes to the bed and sits. He just looks so tired.

So I grab the book and start to read to him. After an hour, I hear his even breaths and realize that he has fallen asleep. I sit and run my hands through his hair, so soft and shiny. Even in sleep, he looks in pain. Poor Damian, I wish there was a way to help him. I have only stopped reading for a minute when he becomes restless. "Shh, it's okay, Damian, I'm here." He stops.

He has said that he loves the sound of my voice but I was not expecting this. When he begins to get restless again, I start to read and he falls back into as restful of a sleep as he can. Well, I am going to need to remember that bit of information. I do not stop reading until Danny comes in with the phone around 10. Today is the last day that I can talk to my parents so Cornelius lets me talk a little longer.

The conversation started out as the same thing: how the greenhouses are coming along, who stopped at the stand, and so on. Then Mom tells me that Sam had stopped by last night, and I get a pang of guilt. I never called Sam before we left, I didn't know what to say to her. How do you tell someone you're not only a witch but that you are dating a nearly 500-hundred-year-old vampire?

"What did you tell her, Mom?"

"The same thing I told the school, we are going out of town for a family emergency. When she stopped by yesterday to drop off your school work, I told her that you were out picking things up but forgot your phone."

"What am I going to do, Mom? How am I going to explain this to her? She is my best friend; I don't want to lose her."

"You won't lose her, Serena, but you can't tell her any of this. It is not safe for everyone involved. Some things are better left as secrets. Listen, honey, it is hard enough finding out about being a witch and needing to keep that from friends. You now have the added burden of keeping the fact that you are dating a vampire a secret. I don't know how to tell you to handle it, but you cannot tell her," she says in a sad voice. I know that she is right but it still hurts. Sam has always been there for me, to not have her to talk to about Damian, is torture. "I am sorry, Serena, but this is how it has to be. This side of your life has to be kept secret from her and everyone else. That doesn't mean that you can't tell her about you and Damian, you just can't tell her that he is a vampire and that he is your soul mate come to you because of a spell."

"Yeah, and even if I could, it sounds crazy. I am living it and it still sounds crazy," I say. Mom and I get off the phone a few minutes later.

I go back to sit with Damian on the bed after having gotten up to pace around the room when on the phone with mom and dad.

So I can tell Sam about Damian. I can tell her how sweet he is, how funny he is, how considerate he is. But I can't tell her anything about his life.

After a few minutes, Damian begins to stir again, this time I let him wake. It is almost time for lunch anyway. At least some food will help him, I hope. He doesn't open his eyes, just rolls over onto his hands and knees, and breathes deep. He lifts his head and looks at me. The pain in his beautiful eyes runs right through my heart.

"My mom called," I say, trying to get his mind off of it.

"Oh? What did you talk about?" His voice no longer the smooth melted chocolate but tight and strained sounding. Like chocolate steal, still a sweet sound, but with a hard tone that he is clearly trying to cover. Where do I come up with these things?

"Nothing much, Sam stopped by last night to drop off my homework," I say, trying to sound like it isn't bothering me. Of course I fail. I suck at lying, which is why this is going to be so hard with Sam. Well, one of the reasons why.

"Serena, you don't have a choice but to lie to her. It isn't safe to tell anyone what we are." I open my mouth to talk but he sees me and keeps going. "I know you think she would understand, but really, you can't know that for sure and it is better to not take the chance." He is right of course, but it still hurts.

"I am going to have to work on my lying skills then because I suck at it," I say in a pouty, put-out voice that makes him smile.

"It is one of the things that I love about you," he says, turning himself the rest of the way to sit on the bed leaning against the wall. "Come here." I walk over and crawl onto the bed to settle next to him. "I know that Sam is your best friend, I don't want you to lose her either, but by lying you are not just protecting us and everyone we love, it is protecting her too."

"I know, it's just that I have never kept anything from her, I have always told her everything. It is going to be hard to keep something so big and so...important to me, from her. She's family."

"I know," he says, laying a kiss in my hair.

"Is it hard being around me right now?" I ask.

"A little. I can smell the blood in your veins but it is weird, normally it would be calling to me."

"It's not, though?"

"No, it is a little like seeing a delicious piece of cake but being too full to eat. I smell your blood and my body cringes away from it."

"Do I smell bad?" I ask as I pinch up my nose and smell my shirt.

He laughs before he cringes a little in pain. A second later, Danny comes in with our food followed by Cornelius, carrying my backpack.

"Your parents dropped this off last night for you. They said that being locked in a room with a hungry, soon-to-be raging vampire is no excuse to fall behind in your last year in high school. I agreed of course," he says in answer to my look of utter confusion as he brings it over to me with a smile.

"You find this funny, don't you?" I ask with a severe lack of interest and a clear look that says I do not appreciate the description of Damian's current or future state. Which of course gets an even bigger smile from Cornelius.

"I find it funny that your parents think you will be able to focus while he is like this. Not while he is and will be in so much pain."

"Your lack of faith in me is alarming," I say going through my bag. "Ugh! Math, I hate math!" I say while pulling out my Accounting book; Cornelius actually laughs.

I look up at him to see that he is smiling at Damian. I look over to Damian to see him trying very hard not to laugh. "Really, you two?" Then I hear Danny giggle from the door. "What is so funny?"

It is Danny who answers, "You said that with just *so* much hatred. I did not realize that a person could actually hate an object with so much force."

"Fine! Yes, I am horrible at math, my dirty little secret," I say, zipping my bag back up.

"I can help you, it will keep me distracted," Damian says, adjusting himself so he is comfortable but can also reach the food to eat.

"That is so sweet, thank you, but no one can help me. I am hopeless when it comes to numbers."

"We will see."

Cornelius says his goodbyes and follows Danny out.

"Are you really that bad or do you just not like math?" Damian asks in between bites.

"No, I am really that bad," I say in complete misery.

"A challenge. This should be fun," he says with a smile as he pops a grape in his mouth.

"I am starting to question this spell's accuracy." I whisper to myself. He laughs.

After lunch, Damian tells me to get my workbook out so we can start. I cringe and try to talk him into history homework, or a book, or a make-out session. That had him pause and I thought he would give in. But he doesn't, dammit.

"So what do you have trouble with?" he asks.

"Anything and everything I can't count on my hands," I answer, which makes him laugh and then moan in pain.

After taking a few deep breaths through the pain, he looks at me.

"Oh, you aren't kidding."

"No, no I'm not. I don't know why. I work really hard, study for hours. Even stay late with the teachers for one-on-one, and I still just can't get it. I swear my brain is wired different or something."

"Okay, well, let's see if we can change that," Damian adjusts himself against the wall and takes out my books. Accounting, ugh, what was I thinking? Well, I was thinking that not taking math to keep up my knowledge of 2+2 would be bad. But is that really worth the headache?

"Are you arguing with yourself?"

"Yes, okay, I am. Are you sure you don't want to just make out? Could be the last time till this is all over," I say giving him a pleading look.

"Don't tempt me."

"But I want to tempt you, I really, really do," I say looking at him from under my lashes. I am not very good with flirting and I am sure I look like an idiot, but really I am desperate and I am going to look like an idiot anyway. He just gives me a blank look. "Fine, but don't say I didn't warn you."

For the next few hours, Damian tries to teach me how to add 2 and 2. Okay, fine, so we worked on my accounting. He shows some amazing patience, more than a saint ever would. And against all odds, I am starting to get it.

We work until Damian finally threw up his arms. "See, I told you! I knew you would get it," he says this with his lips tight and pain laced in his voice.

"Yes, and I will be amazed and jumping for joy later, right know I am more concerned about you. Damian, you are really in pain, aren't you?" He looks so pale with pain lines around his eyes and lips. "Damian, what can I do?" I ask, knowing the answer already. Aside from coming up with a few bags of blood, there is nothing I can do.

He smiles at me lying his hand on my cheek. "I will be fine, this isn't going to kill me."

"No, just hurt like hell," I say sarcastically.

"Exactly."

I smirk at him, not finding that the least bit funny. The truth is, I think it is hurting me more to see him in pain than it is for him being in pain. If that isn't love, I don't know what is.

Chapter 19

Damian gets off the bed and heads to the bathroom as I finish my accounting. When he comes out, he doesn't come back to the bed but instead goes back to the corner. I leave him be and start on my English paper, knowing that he needs space, as far from me as he can get.

By dinner, he is still in the corner. When Danny comes in with our food, he takes Damian's to the corner for him. Of course, I understand why but that doesn't change the hurt. I want to have him next to me, touching me, laughing with me. Or even at me, I don't care. But for the next few days, none of that is going to happen. I guess it has really started, that is where he is going to stay till all this is over.

I wish I could do *something* but all I can do is keep my distance and try to make this as comfortable as I can. *Okay, don't cry, Serena, just finish your food, grab a book, and read out loud to him, try to get his mind off it.*

And I know just the book. I walk over to the door when I am done eating. "Danny...? Cornelius...?" I yell out. A minute later, Danny comes to the door.

"Do you want me to get your tray?" he asks as he unlocks and opens the door.

"Sure, but that isn't why I called you. Can you get me Alice in Wonderland by Lewis Carroll?" Danny gives me a confused look. "I love that book, it is weird and fun."

He looks me up and down ignoring the low growl from the corner. "Kind of like you" he says with a laugh.

"I knew you would understand," I answer with a smile before smacking is arm. He turns to leave with my cleaned-off tray and Damian's half eaten one. "Hey, Danny?" I ask and he turns to me before closing the door completely. "The pain seems to be getting worse faster now, is that normal?"

"Yes, once his body realized it was getting low on blood and wasn't getting any more, it sent the blood he has into his organs looking for more. He will be fine until the blood goes to his heart and brain to look for more, which won't happen till he becomes desperate." With that he leaves.

"This isn't desperate?" I whisper to myself looking at Damian sitting in the corner with his legs pressed into his chest.

"Stop…looking at me…like that. It is not so bad… I can handle it." With his teeth clenched I have to concentrate to understand what he is saying.

"Yeah, you sound like you are walking through a meadow filled with rainbows and unicorns."

"You know you are just a steaming pile of sunshine when you are being sarcastic," he says to me in my head, giving me a wink.

"Aw, you noticed," I say with a sweet smile. That gets a smile from him, at least he is smiling again. All I want in this world is to go over to him and hold him, tell him that it will be okay, we will get through this.

"Don't, Serena! I can see it in your eyes. Stay over there!" he yells at me. *"Please don't give me that look again. I know and I want nothing more than to hold you, but you have to stay away. Please, I don't want to hurt you! I know that it was fine earlier but now that it has really started, I don't want to take the chance that my body will want your blood."*

"Isn't the whole point of this to show that you won't, you can't," I say, taking a step to him. Don't ask me why, because I don't know, but I have to tempt fate. Oh, I know, *"Wouldn't it be better for you to get used to me while like this? Wouldn't it make it easier for you to deal with it later?"* I ask, damn near pleading with him. All he does is stare at me quizzically as I wait for him to make up his mind. To just give in to what we both want, and what we both need. Before he can answer, Danny bangs on the door, making me jump, which of course makes him laugh. Great, I have created a monster. He pokes the book through the bars on the door.

"That was fast," I say coming over and taking the book. I open to the cover page and my mouth drops to the floor. "You have got to be kidding! A first addition? Signed? How in the hell did you get this so fast?"

"Turns out, it is one of Cornelius's favorites," Danny answers with a laugh as he walks away.

"Well, that I didn't see coming." I turn to look at Damian as he says that. *"Okay, fine you can come sit with me and read."* I was already to him before the second word left his lips, which makes him laugh, which makes him groan.

"Stop laughing, you keep hurting yourself," I scowl.

"Stop being funny." I see that it is too much work to speak so I point to my head. *"Yes, I know."*

"So you didn't know that this was one of Cornelius's favorite books?" I ask turning to the first page.

"I don't know everything about the man."

"What is your favorite book?" I ask before starting.

"In Cold Blood?" I just stare at him until he laughs in my head. *"Okay fine,* Sherlock Holmes.*"*

"Now that I can see." I laugh at him and begin to read. The book of Alice in Wonderland is not much like the movie. It is a little crazier and told through Alice's eyes. Sometimes it is hard to figure out what exactly is going on. But that is why I love it. Lewis Carroll takes ordinary boring life and makes it fun, and unique, if not a bit, well, mad. Damian lays down with his head on my lap and relaxes.

I read to him while running my hand through his hair, enjoying the soft tendrils until finally Damian falls asleep. Not necessarily restful, but at least he is sleeping. So I levitate a pillow to me and lay him down; being a witch sure does come in handy.

I hurry over to the bathroom and clean up before lying down for a fitful night of no sleep. How could I possibly sleep while all I hear is Damian moaning? Tomorrow is going to be worse and it is going to kill me to see it.

Chapter 20
Monday, Day 4

By midnight I am so tired and so ready to cry. Wait... *"Damian... it's okay. Breath, I am right here with you. Ignore the pain and focus on my voice."* I keep talking to him, keep repeating that I am right here and before long, he calms. After a half an hour, his long agonizing moans become nothing more than clenched teeth and a low moan here and there.

He will be alright this night but what of tomorrow night? Will I be able to soothe him? Will I be able to break through the fog of pain?

More importantly, when will his pain be enough to satisfy the Council? What will happen after all this? Will the Council take our word for it? Cornelius believes us, but he knows Damian would never lie to him, not about something like this. After a few hours, I can't take it. All the questions are beginning to drive me crazy.

I get up and go to the door. "Danny?" I call out. I know that someone is there, I suppose it is just hopeful thinking that it will be Danny. I mean, it is the middle of the night, Danny wouldn't still be here. Before anyone answers or comes to the door, I hear Damian moan, *"Shh, I am still here, breathe, I am not going anywhere."*

When I turn back, it is to see a larger man, maybe six foot four inches. Is there a height requirement to become a vampire; what is it for girls, I wonder. Off subject here, I take a closer look at him and see that he has broad shoulders and shaggy brown hair that goes past his shoulder blades. "What can I do for you?" he asks in a surprisingly high-pitched voice. I mean it is not as high as a woman's voice but seriously… wow.

He opens the door as I ask "Um…who are you?"

"Geffrey, with a G. I am your night guard." And with that, I nearly lose all sense. It takes everything, every ounce of control that I have, which really is not a lot, not to fall to the floor laughing so hard I pee myself. That would be the stupidest thing I could do. To laugh in the face of a very large vampire who could easily kill me while I am too busy laughing at his high-pitched voice and preppy name. He has got to win so many fights by starting out with that. I mean really, all he would have to do is go up to his enemy and say, 'Hi my name is Geffrey, with a G,' and then kill them while they laugh.

I look up to see that Geffrey with a G is looking down at me as if I have lost my mind. Oh right, he is waiting for me to answer. I make sure to compose myself before opening my mouth. "I was wondering if it is at all possible to speak with Cornelius?" I tend to get very formal while trying not to offend someone or burst out into hysterics, it would seem.

"I am not sure, let me find out, can I tell him what this is about?" Okay, so apparently, he is going to follow suit and be extra sweet. Or maybe this is how he actually speaks, wouldn't that make him an extra bundle of funny. This guy is too much!

"Um, well, I just have a few questions that I would appreciate his opinion on."

"Very well, I will tell him." With that, Geffrey with a G, leaves. I turn around and start back to speaking to Damian. *"It's okay, baby. All will be okay."*

Twenty minutes later, Cornelius walks in, and I try to play it cool for all of twenty seconds. "Thank all that is holy," I say running up to him, "I can't take this, I…I just can't. You have to do something, look at him!" I plead.

I turn and look at Damian who is beginning to shake. "Cornelius, he is in so much pain. There has to be something that you can do. I can't watch him in this much pain!" With that I lose it. Right in front of Cornelius, I break down and cry. Damian has only been in true pain for one day and I can't stay strong enough to deal with that. How sad am I, how pathetic am I? What kind of soul mate am I to a vampire that after one day of him being in pain, I break down?

Cornelius grabs me and brings me in for a hug. Damian must not have been asleep after all because out of nowhere he has me across the room and Cornelius on the floor, fangs out and about to rip out his throat.

"Damian! Enough!" I shout.

With his hand still around Cornelius's neck, Damian turns and looks into my eyes, but he is not there.

"Damian…" I say walking slowly over to him, "baby, listen to me. Cornelius was not trying to hurt me, or steal me from you. Please…look at me, come back." His eyes

166

begin to clear, but only for a moment before the pain comes back. With the last bit of sense and strength he has, he jumps back from Cornelius.

"Serena," he says with such longing and sorrow that my heart breaks a little, with that he falls crying out in pain, grabbing his head.

"Damian!" I throw out my arms, too far to catch him but he never hits the floor. Seriously, this witch thing has its perks. Not the point right now!

"Cornelius, please, there has to be something you can do," I say as I put him on the bed.

"He just did it."

"What?" Not going to lie, that came out a little dumbfounded and a bit slow. It's not my fault. Between sleep deprivation and worrying out of my damn mind and now my own monologue is starting to sound hysterical.

"He just came out of a pain-induced fog, not to mention I believe he was sleeping when I walked in, all to protect you. I will show this video to the Council. But remember, Serena, there is no guarantee." He looks at Damian and then turns and leaves.

I stand there looking from the door to Damian. *"Damian? Baby, how are you doing?"*

"Just wonderful, I feel like I am lying on a fluffy cloud being kissed by angels."

"Well now, there is no need for the sarcasm, but I am glad that you still have your humor."

"Sorry...and I am sorry about losing it there for a minute."

"I'm not, I told you that you wouldn't hurt me."

"That won't be enough for them, Serena," he says groaning out loud.

"I know, Damian, but it's a start."

He tried to get back to sleep but it just was not going to happen. No matter how much I talked to him.

"Serena, why don't you try to get some sleep? I can move back to my corner so I stop shaking the bed."

"Yeah, that sounds great, my sending you to a corner so I can sleep." Damian laughs but rolls off the bed and crawls to the corner. *"Damian, I am fine, get back on the bed."*

"You are far from fine, even your voice in my head is slurred. It is 4 in the morning, get some sleep."

"I am still better off than you, so get back over here."

"Not the point, you have a chance of sleep I do not. So sleep."

"Fine, mister bossy pants."

"That's real mature," he laughs in my head.

"Thank you, I thought so." I yawn, snuggling into the pillow.

He laughs. *"I love you."*

"I love you, too," I say before I drift off to sleep.

When I wake up a few hours later, it is to loud groaning. "Damian!" I shoot up in bed and turn to see him in a fetal position in the corner, grabbing at his head. *"Damian, can you hear me?"*

"Serena? It is getting really bad. My head feels like it is being axed!"

I get up and run to the door. "Danny! Danny!"

"I'm going, Serena. I'll get Cornelius."

"Thank you," I whisper after him. I take a deep breath and turn back to Damian. I run over to him when I see he is starting to rip at his hair. "Damian, no," I say, but when I notice that his fangs are out, I get really concerned. "How long have your fangs been out, Damian? Can you get them back in?"

"They have been out since you fell asleep. I can't get them back in. I am so hungry, Serena. They are never going to let me out. This is a good enough reason to them to let me die in here."

"Cornelius will never let that happen."

"How long have you been able to read his thoughts?" I jump, spinning around to face the angry voice of Cornelius Gray. I am not sure why, but Cornelius has malice written all over him. What really gets me though is that I never heard the lock slide, never heard the door open, but here he is.

"Damian?"

"Go ahead and tell him."

"Are you sure? You didn't want anyone to know that we can do this."

"He will find out eventually anyway, he clearly knows something is up and is suspicious of it. It is safer for you if you just tell him."

"Okay." To Cornelius I say, "I can't read his thoughts, I can only hear him when he sends it to me. All soul mates of witches can do it. He can hear mine as well." He just looks at me, then to Damian.

"Okay," he says finally. "The Council has decided that more proof is needed."

I was expecting that but still, it makes me angry. "Damian is right, they are going to let him die in here and be justified in doing so."

"I am afraid so and there is nothing I can do unless I want an uproar on my hands." Now I am furious. Without thinking, my hands light up in fire that begins to travel up my arms.

How dare he? Damian gave up a life for him, was willing to become Grand Master for him. All he can say is there is nothing he can do!

"Are you really ready to take me on? To take on the Vampire Council for him?" I can hear the mirth in his voice. Is he really being condescending to me? Way to piss me off even more! I begin to float up into the air, my hair blowing and rising to look like flames in the wind. I can hear my power snap as my anger rises.

"What do you think?" I say in the most aggressive and violent voice that has ever passed through my lips. I can hear Damian in my head telling me to stop, to just let them kill him and walk out of here. There is no way I am doing that. I will die trying to save him before I ever let that happen.

Chapter 21

Then Cornelius smiles. "That is what I wanted to hear, and frankly, see. You truly are amazing, Serena. Your mother told me so but I wanted to see it."

That has me dropping to the ground. "What?" I really need to work at staying in character when I am trying to be tough because that, once again, came out dumbfounded. "My mother told you? Is this all a game to you?"

"No, this is not a game to me. I am not going to allow those pretentious asses kill Damian because he fell in love with someone they do not approve of. He has proven himself to me, this *is* real. Unfortunately, I cannot let him go without an uprising in the wake, because no doubt Bernard will start one. The others would not have the nerve to, but he does. After I left you this morning, I called the Council to my office. I showed them the surveillance footage and explained the eyes and everything else; they said that no amount of proof would be enough, Damian broke a law and must die. After they left, I paced my office trying to think of how to stop this. Finally, I called your parents." He walks over to Damian and pulls out a blood bag.

"Cornelius, the cameras," I say, knowing that the Council will see this.

"Don't worry, I have disabled the cameras temporarily. Now listen, Serena, this is what you must do. This one bag will get his body to stop attacking itself for maybe two hours. He will still be in immense pain but at least functional. You have called me down here to demand to see the Council," he says this getting up and giving me a sharp look. Okay, message received loud and clear. "I will get them here but you are going to have to fight, Serena."

"No," Damian says, his voice sounding gravelly after not talking for so long, and still being in pain doesn't help.

"Damian, you are not strong enough, and even with my help, we cannot take on all six," Cornelius says, "I hate to admit it but we need the witch's help."

"I will help." We all turn towards the door to see Danny.

"Thank you, Danny, but no. I do not want anyone else involved. If this goes bad, I do not want the Council to then kill you for helping," Cornelius says.

"I like Serena, I will do what I can to help her."

"Aw, come here you big pooh bear," I say walking to him.

"Serena…" Danny says, giving me a look of warning.

"Oh right, sorry, you big deadly vampire pooh bear."

"Thank you," he says giving me a hug. I hear the low growl behind me.

"Ignore him."

Damian grunts, "He is just lucky I have a pint in me or he would be dead right now."

"Danny, if something happens to Damian, you can take Serena and run," Cornelius says after seeing that Danny wants to help in some way and is not going to give up.

"I will. Thank you, sir."

"Hey, in case anyone was wondering, I can take care of myself."

"Yes, you can. Your mother told me that you have been showing enormous talent, seeing as the first night you conjured fire. Damian will worry if there isn't a backup plan for your safety though."

"I will worry anyway," Damian says as he stands and comes to me.

"It's okay, I will worry about you too," I say as I stretch up to kiss him. "Welcome back."

Damian smiles at me as Cornelius moves back towards the door. "The Council will come down and you will have to be ready, Serena." He looks at me with remorse. I understood; with any luck in the world, I will not have to take a life today, but I need to be ready to do so. If I am being honest with myself, I never will. For any reason.

Cornelius leaves, locking the door behind him. We do not move, but instead stand there as if ready for the flood gates to open. I know what I am thinking about, whether we will make it out of this with both our lives. I am not ready for this, maybe it was naive, but I really was starting to think that this would end okay. That the Council would see the love between us as well as the fact that Damian never made a move for my blood. I guess I didn't want to see just how much the Council hates Damian, even though he told me as much, many times.

I just never thought it was too much to ask that we could live in peace. To be together without someone telling us we can't. In reality, every couple has at least one person who doesn't want them together. Take Sam and I; we don't want Sara and James together. Normally, people don't try to kill the couple though. Welcome to my life.

"Okay, let's just try to talk to them first."

"You really think that is going to work? The mere fact that you are able to stand right now will give away that something isn't right," I say looking to Damian.

He is quiet for a moment. Looking down at me as he smiles and my heart skips a beat. "It is a good thing both of us aren't blood deprived." I can't help but laugh. Damian lets go of my hand and cups my face, moving to stand in front of me. "I love you so much, so how about you don't do anything too dangerous, okay?"

"No guarantees, but I will try." He rolls his beautiful blue and green eyes at me. "I love you, Damian, I will do whatever I have to in order to keep you alive. Besides, I was promised a soul mate and I am going to keep you, no refunds." He laughs as he leans down to kiss me.

It is the moment our lips meet that I hear the lock on the door slide. It is the moment that my eyes close that I hear the door open. It is the moment I realize what Damian is doing that I hear footsteps enter our little cell. His fangs slide out slowly.

He has finally realized that he will not hurt me. *"Do it,"* I send to him. He smiles against my lips pulling back slightly. Then so fast that I don't even feel it, he slices my lip. With painstaking slowness, he licks the single drop of blood so that all of the Council can see.

They all gasp. "I knew he lied," I hear one of them say. A tall slender man that looks to be in his late forties. Though I know he is much older.

"That's Bernard. If we kill any of them today, it has to be him." Damian pulls back from me and looks to the Council. *"They are more surprised that I pulled away than anything. At this level of need after tasting fresh blood, I should not be able to. We have their attention now,"* he says grabbing my hand. He is right, I can see it in their eyes. All but Bernard, he simply looks angry.

"That is not possible! She has done something to him that is the only way," Bernard yells.

"And what exactly could I have done? I have only had my powers for five days. How am I supposed to know how to do something that big?"

"You are a Rae, I would not put anything past you," Bernard sneers at me.

"I feel the need to say thank you as well as smack you. Very conflicted right now," I say, Damian smirks.

"I am glad you have called us down here, Damian. Now we can see quite clearly that you have been playing a game. The witch has cut off your pain and is somehow controlling you. No matter, we will end this now. Don't you all agree?" Bernard says in a voice that clearly says he thinks he is more superior. As well as in control.

They all nod but one. "I do not believe so, look at their eyes. No spell can do that that I have ever seen." She is a tall, sleek woman that looks like a walking skeleton. Seriously, lady, gain some weight.

"Then you are a fool, Vanessa. Clearly the eyes are a sign of her control."

175

"Don't ever call me a fool again, Bernard," Vanessa says turning on him, her face in his; dang she is tall! "Never in my six hundred years have I seen eyes like theirs. Two separate, distinctive colors merging together. You cannot tell me that you do not see Damian's eye color in there and I am assuming that the green in yours, Serena?" she asks turning to me.

"Yes." Oh, I like her. In a blink she is in front of me and Damian has her by the neck.

"Her lip, Damian, look at her lip," she squeaks out. I turn to look at Damian; he is staring at my lip. As he brings his hand to my lip, I feel Vanessa hit the floor at my feet.

"What? What's wrong?" I ask, my hand going to my lip as well. Then I feel it, or the lack of it. My lip is no longer sliced. I should have known something was up since it no longer stung but I was a little preoccupied. "What does that mean?" I ask looking at Damian.

"You healed like a vampire," he whispers. His eyes hold both shock and joy.

"More proof she is connected to him, controlling him, taking from him in some way, and he is allowing it. A witch cannot heal like a vampire any other way!" Bernard says while the rest of the Council nods. Well, all but Vanessa. She simply looks in awe.

Damian turns on him. "Did any of you even watch any of the surveillance footage?"

"Of course we did," Bernard says, looking down his nose at Damian and speaking as if he is offended he even asked.

"Really? Well, if you actually had, you would have seen just how far our connection goes." With that Damian brings two fireballs into his hands. Then he does something I haven't seen him do. He spreads the fire to cover his hands.

"When did you learn to do that?"

"Just now."

"That is so good! I am so proud of you!"

"Well, you are a good teacher," Damian says, never taking his eyes off Bernard.

"I didn't teach you that."

"Okay, so I am a good watcher." I can't help but laugh. But when I look over to Bernard, I see why Damian is keeping his eyes on him. Bernard is angry and my humor comes to a very quick death.

"That is not possible," Bernard says in a low voice. Shit.

"You are forgetting something. Love is the most powerful thing in the world. You can try to deny it all you want, but what Damian and I have is real, and there is nothing you can do that will stop us from leaving here," I say with a burst of bravery and let's face it, hope. So to get my point across, I stir up a gust of wind causing their hair to billow and their clothes to tighten around them. They pay no attention. Tough crowd.

"Here, you are forgetting something, Serena Rae. Damian is blood deprived, making him very weak. Do you really think that you and you alone can beat all of us?"

"Not all of us, I believe they are telling the truth and I will not stand in their way. Not this day." With that Vanessa leaves. Well, that is kind of sad, the least she could do is help. Then a miracle; the last four bow to Damian, then turn and leave.

"The decision has been made, Bernard," Cornelius says, not even trying to hide his relief.

"Once again, your golden child wins, surprise, surprise." He turns to leave, keeping Damian in his sight.

"Damian..."

"I see, but I am too weak, Serena, I have all I can to stay standing right now." In a split second, Bernard lunges and I know what I have to do. Time to try what I have been wondering since learning about us literally being connected. I can feel the energy flowing out of him to me and vice versa. Time to see if I can push more energy into him from me. I close my eyes and push all the energy I can muster and send it to him across our connection. My eyes snap open in time to see Damian's color come back and Bernard slam into him. He hasn't had time to fully recover yet. I reach out and grab Bernard with my magic and new vampire strength. I pull Bernard from him, sending him across the room.

"Serena, what did you do?" Damian asks as he gets up and flexes.

"I am sending you my energy, so you better end this fast because I don't know how long I can keep it up, I am pretty sleep deprived."

"As long as you are here to help, I think I can do that. Thank you." In a flash, Bernard is up; Damian spins to miss the missile that is Bernard and shoves him to the wall, causing it to crack. Blood pours down his face.

"Now it will be over in no time." I glance quickly to Cornelius and back as he steps up to stand next to me.

"What makes you say that?"

"Blood, my dear, Serena. Yours may not affect him but all others do. Good thing too because you do not look so good." Just as he says that, I see Damian change. His fangs extend, his eyes begin to glow, and he looks the predator he

178

truly is. For the first time, Bernard looks afraid. "What did you do, Serena? How is he fine?" I hear Cornelius ask as if nothing is going on in front of us.

"Nothing, I am just sending him energy," I say absently.

"Stop, Serena."

"Why?" I ask as Bernard begins to beg and Damian forms a fireball. Apparently, he has enough sense to just put the man out of his misery, and frankly, I do not want to see the blood bath that would surely be if he chose to feed instead.

"Because you are beginning to slur your words." Damian throws the fireball, causing Bernard to be engulfed in flames. The screams echo throughout the room. Without warning, my legs give out and Damian is there holding me. "Enough, Serena!" Cornelius yells just as everything goes black.

Chapter 22

I wake up with a strange feeling of peace, I haven't felt at peace in days. I stretch, smiling and enjoying the softness of my sheets. Wait...my sheets? My eyes fly open and I jump up to see my bedroom. What happened? Why am I here? Oh...my...God, was it all a dream? No, no, no, no! It would be like me to dream something like that up. To dream up someone so perfect, so hot, so...ugh! I drop back down to my bed. Why do I insist on torturing myself? Of course I would dream up the prefect guy just because I can and then end up spending the rest of my life comparing every guy I meet to him. Then I will die alone with my twenty cats all named Fluffernutter just so I don't forget one.

What is wrong with me? That sounded very close to whiny in my head.

"I can feel your mind running a mile a minute." At the sound of his voice in my head, I jump, landing on my butt on the floor next to my bed. Before I can even register what just happened, he is in front of me.

"Damian!?" I say grabbing his arms and squeezing to make sure he is in fact real.

"Yes?" he says, dragging it out. "Are you okay?" He looks at me, worried.

"Yes, the last thing I remember is Bernard in flames, then I wake up in my bed. I was worried I had dreamed the whole thing," I say getting up.

"You must have one active imagination then," he says smiling at me.

"Har-har." He chuckles at me.

"Okay, what happened?"

"Walk with me," he says grabbing my hand. He pulls me out of my bedroom to the patio and right to our bench. Sitting down, he pats the seat for me to sit next to him. He takes my hands. "Okay, Bernard is dead and the Council has agreed to let us be, for now."

"What do you mean for now?"

"Well, they agree that we cannot fight this and that we truly are in love. But the fact that I so easily was able to kill Bernard being so blood deprived, has them worried that us together is dangerous. What you did scared them. Speaking of...Cornelius is not happy with you."

"Again, why?"

"You really scared him, you scared me. Serena, you almost died."

"What? No... how? I didn't do anything." He cups my face and looks deep into my eyes. Then I see it, the fear that he had been hiding. "Oh, Damian, I am so sorry."

"Serena, I would have died if you hadn't given me your energy. But you didn't think about the fact that I was nearly completely drained. I needed a lot, so you couldn't stop. I nearly killed you."

"No, you did not. I knew what I was doing, I knew you needed a lot but it didn't matter. I was not going to let you die. I am just glad you ended it quickly. Now why is Cornelius mad?"

"Because you nearly died!" he yells, throwing his hands up.

"Really? Aw, he does care."

"You had Danny worried too, he sent you flowers, they're on the table." He smiles and my heart melts.

I give my head a shake as he laughs. "So how long have I been out?" It must have been a while since everyone is freaking out.

He looks at his watch. "Two hours." What?

I grab his wrist and look, one pm. It is still Monday, it has only been two hours since the Council came to us in the cell. "How is that possible?" I whisper. He drags my eyes up to look at him.

"I have a theory."

I laugh. "Of course you do." He smiles and I stop breathing. Dang, that is never going to end.

"Serena, your lip healed." At the reminder my hand goes to my lip. "Then you recover in two hours from near death. You were barely breathing, you were blue, and I really thought you were dead. Never again do I want to go through that, got it?"

"You're getting off track here, sexy."

"Sorry. Serena, those are things a vampire can do. I think you might...well, it is possible you also got..."

"Don't joke with me right now, Damian, not about this! You really think I might be immortal? I don't have to lose you?" I ask, hope growing in my heart.

"There is only one way to truly test it and I am not willing to nearly kill you again, so I am going with, time will tell, but I really do think so."

I cup his face and with the most stern voice and look, I say, "You did not nearly kill me, so stop." Then with a smile, I jump onto his lap and kiss him with everything I have. I have been worrying about that in the back of my head. I tried not to think of it, but it always crept up. Thank all that is holy I don't have to anymore.

We sit on the bench talking and kissing for hours. I learned all about his family. That his father was a blacksmith and taught Damian how to craft his own sword. How his mom would have to make mitten after mitten every winter because he would always lose them. That his parents died only months apart when he was 16 from the influenza. That Cornelius found him dying at 19 in his father's blacksmith shop that he had taken over and saved him.

His life story tells you more than anything who Damian is. How much he loved his parents. How proud he was that he was able to take over for his father and carry on the family's reputation. How grateful to Cornelius he is for saving him from dying the same way as his parents. But mostly, how alone he has felt all his life. Never again will he feel that way.

My parents come over to us on the bench with plates full of sandwiches for dinner and a blanket. We all sit under the tree eating. "Cornelius called," my mom says.

"Well, you guys have become close during our lock-up," I say smiling. I am glad they have; Cornelius means a lot to Damian, and really to me too now. I want my parents to like Damian's surrogate dad of sorts.

"He is a very nice man, honey, and cares deeply for Damian. Anyway, he says he will be stopping in later to check on you."

"Did you tell him I am fine, there is no need to waste a trip up here?"

"He wants to, Serena," my dad says, and I shrug and take a bite of my sandwich. I didn't taste it though. I get this wave of feeling that I can't shake. Something is coming.

"What's wrong?"

"Nothing...I just feel like something big is about to happen."

After dinner, my parents go back to work in the greenhouses while Damian and I spend the rest of the day walking around the garden talking. We are on our way back to the house when he stops me. "What is it, Serena? Something has been bothering you all day."

"Same old, same old. I am just sad that I can't tell Sam anything about you, about us."

"Yes, you can, just not the vampire witch stuff."

"That's just it, Damian, I have to lie. I can't tell her that your parents died without her wondering who you lived with. Or where. I can't tell her where I was all weekend. I can't tell her how it is that I love you so much when the lie is that I haven't seen you since Thursday. Even if I could tell her that I saw you all weekend, it still wouldn't make sense to her that I fell in love with you so quickly. I am not good at lying, Damian, especially to Sam. She sees right through me." He pulls me into a hug and I instantly relax into him. I take a deep breath of his woodsy scent and immediately feel at home.

"I know and I am sorry it has to be this way, you do understand why, right?"

"Yes, I understand and I won't say anything."

"I am sorry, it will be okay though, I promise," he says kissing the top of my head.

After a few minutes, we continue our walk to the house. I stop at the table to smell the lilies that Danny sent me. My deadly vampire pooh bear. He may be big and scary but he is a sweetheart.

"So what should we make for dessert?" Damian asks from the kitchen.

"How about spaghetti?"

He looks at me as I round the island that divide the kitchen and dining room to stand next to him. "First, for dessert? Second, you can't cook, can you?" he smiles.

"See, learning new things about each other all the time. Feels good, doesn't it?" He laughs as he leans down and kisses me, causing my legs to get weak and him to lift me up and set me on the counter. "Stay," he says pointing to me and giving me a stern look. I laugh as he walks away and starts getting everything around. I watch captivated at how smooth his movements are. He really is magnificent. I unknowingly lick my lips and he stops. Turning to me, I see the green in his eyes brighten. I smile sweetly.

"Stop it," he says in that gravelly, low voice that makes my stomach do somersaults every time I hear it.

"Stop what?"

"Evil little witch, or really this time you are my evil little vixen," he says, turning back to his task. I try not to laugh.

"So you don't even know how to make spaghetti?" he asks, trying to change the subject. What he doesn't realize is that he has added to it.

"It's the only thing I can make," I say looking around at anything but him. He spins around and looks at me.

"Oh, you are good," he says coming toward me. I burst out laughing. When he reaches me, he grabs hold of the nape of my neck and pulls me to him for an earthquake of a kiss. When he pulls away, I cannot breathe and I am fully aware that my eyes are glowing as bright as a lighthouse. "So why would you make me think you can't even make spaghetti?"

"Because I wanted to watch you move around the kitchen. I like to watch your butt. You have a *nice* butt." That makes him laugh.

"My God, I love you. Okay, you can watch but next time I watch and you cook," he says walking away.

"If you remember correctly, I did tell you I wanted to take a cooking class. That somewhat implies that I can't cook," I say as he puts all the fixings for chocolate chip cookies next to me.

"Yes, you did, maybe we can go to Italy and take a class," he says, leaning over to kiss me before going back to cracking the eggs.

"Really?"

"Sure, unless you want to go to France, or Spain. Anything you want."

"You are the most amazing man ever, you know that?" He smiles at me. I jump from the counter and go over to him. "I love you."

"I love you, too," he says, wrapping me in his arms and kissing me sweetly.

We talk about this and that as we finish cooking. When the hot-out-of-the-oven cookies are on the table, we go out front to tell my parents that dessert is done. As soon as we step off the porch, Cornelius pulls in. "I should go get another glass of milk for him," I say as I turn to head in, but Damian grabs my arm.

"You might want to wait a minute." I turn in time to see Sam pull in and park next to Cornelius just as he is getting out. Cornelius walks around the front of his car as Sam jumps out, her hands full of what looks like homework.

"Serena, you're back!" she yells as she starts to run around the car... right into Cornelius. The papers in her arms go flying as she starts to fall. Cornelius quickly catches her to him. He holds her closely as they look at each other, stunned. No one says anything for a moment as they stare into each other's eyes as if in a romantic comedy. My life has seriously become a movie.

"Wow," Sam breathes.

"You took the word right out of my mouth," Cornelius whispers. I can see the look in his eyes. He is enthralled and absolutely smitten. I look to Sam to see that she may not be breathing. Oh honey, I know the feeling, and that will not fade. I still feel like I can't breathe when Damian looks at me, or smiles, or laughs, or speaks. I feel the need to get an inhaler.

"What is happening?" Damian asks. I smile as I realize what this truly means.

"The solution to both of our problems," I say. I cannot help but laugh a little as Damian wraps his arms around me.

"And what problems are they? I did not realize we had any problems."

"Well, we do and they just solved themselves, which is funny since, in a way, they were the problem."

"Again, those problems would be?"

"You not wanting to be Grand Master and me not wanting to lie to Sam."

"You think them staring at each other is the answer?"

"Absolutely," I say leaning into his chest, *"look at them, Damian, their worlds just shook."* I smile as we watch Cornelius and Sam fluster their way around, picking up the dropped papers. *"They are perfect, Damian, like you and me. Two halves of one soul."*

"Oh right, what was it you said to me, souls together?" Damian spins me around and kisses me till my heart skips a beat and I stop breathing and my world once again shakes.

CPSIA information can be obtained
at www.ICGtesting.com
Printed in the USA
BVHW040159030521
606318BV00014B/784

9 781641 823616